THE SANDLOT PROMISE

THE SANDLOT PROMISE

A Story of Mills, Families, and the Fence That Held

Book One of The Sandlot Series

WALTER A. BEEDE

Beede Baseball Publishing LLC

Dedication

For the men and women who worked the lines at GE,
who came home with metal in their lungs
and hope in their pockets,
and for the kids who learned to dream
under the sound of the whistle.
And in memory of
Officer Arthur Belmonte
of the Saugus Police Department,
who lost his life on the night of
December 27, 1969,
and of Officer Frederick Forni,
who survived that night and
carried its wounds forward.
— Walter A. Beede

The Sandlot Series

Prequel: Beneath the Home Run Sky

Book One: The Sandlot Promise

Book Two: The Sandlot Legacy

Book Three: The Sandlot Spirit

Series Note

Beneath the Home Run Sky is a Sandlot Series Prequel. It tells the earlier story of Fred Davis, George Davis, Mary Davis, Cedarbrook Field, and the first lines pulled across the dirt.

The Sandlot Promise begins after that older field already carries memory. What changes here is the fence: the line raised after loss, meant to reclaim the field for children and give the town something straight to hold.

Foreword

by Bret Saberhagen

This book isn't about the big leagues. It's about a small New England town, a frozen creek. And a fence that gets built board by board, nail by nail, at a time when everything else seems to be coming apart. It's about a family trying to hang on to its faith and its decency after the kind of tragedy that leaves an empty chair at the table and a permanent ache in the room.

Baseball is the backdrop here, but it's also the language. In these pages, you'll see what I've seen in clubhouses and sandlots alike: men and women who've been knocked down more than once, who still show up early, still rake the infield, still make sure a kid's name gets written on a lineup card. You'll recognize the way a fence becomes more than wood and nails. It turns into a boundary for chaos, a promise that—at least on this patch of dirt—the adults are going to do everything they can to keep the worst of the world on the other side.

What struck me most about Walter's story is how honest it is about grief and fear without giving in to either one. He doesn't write in clichés. The people of Saugus aren't perfect. They argue, they doubt, they carry grudges and secrets. Some keep their heads down and hope trouble passes by.

Others decide that hope isn't enough, that if you want decency to survive, you have to build something that will outlast you.

For Fred Davis, that something is a fence. For Mary, it's a ledger, simple lines of handwriting that try to make sense of a world that doesn't always add up. For Jack, it's a field where he learns that being tough doesn't mean going it alone. I've played with and against guys like these my whole life. I've seen what it means when a community rallies around a field, a team, a kid. I've also seen what happens when nobody does.

There's a line that runs through this book—from the Red Coach Grill shooting to the refinery fights, from letters sent home from war to a boy throwing in the cold with more on his shoulders than any teenager should have to carry. It's the same line that runs from the mills to the marshes, from Fenway Park to every little backstop leaning against a patch of grass behind some school or church. If you've ever coached a team, played on one, or sat in the stands with a knot in your throat hoping your kid gets one more at-bat, you'll recognize that line.

Walter writes this story with the eye of a coach, the heart of a parent, and the memory of a kid who spent a lot of time on the far side of a fence, waiting to be invited in. He understands that the real heroes are often the ones who never get their names announced: the person who shovels the baselines after a storm, the neighbor who quietly buys a glove for a kid who can't afford one, the cop or factory worker who spends his only day off hitting ground balls until the sun goes down.

This is a book about them.

It's also a reminder that the lines we draw matter. The lines of a field. The lines in a ledger. The moral lines a town refuses to cross, even when it would be easier—or more profitable—to look away. In an era when youth sports can feel more like business than childhood, The Sandlot Promise pulls us back to a time and place where the game still belonged to kids and the adults were there to protect that.

I'm honored to write this foreword for Walter's story. I hope, as you turn these pages, you'll think about the fences in your own life—the people who built them, the promises they made. And the ways you can keep them straight for the next generation.

Because at the end of the day, championships are great. Rings are great. But the real legacy of this game is found in the small fields, in the kids who fall asleep with dirt still on their socks. And in the ordinary people who decide that, in their corner of the world, decency is going to have a home plate and a chance.

Bret Saberhagen

World Series Champion, Father, and Baseball Lifer

Reflective Prelude — The Last Honest Decade

©

(1969)

MOST MORNINGS BEGAN WITH a knock at the back door. Three quick raps. Then a voice through the screen.

"Hey. You coming out?" In the neighborhoods that ran between Lynn and Saugus, that was enough. A kid could be halfway into his sneakers before his mother answered for him. Screen doors slapped. Bikes hit pavement. Somebody came carrying a bat with no tape left on the handle.

By the time the sun got hold of the street, the day already belonged to whoever showed up. The older boys made the first call. Touch football in the lot if the ground was dry. Stickball if Mr. D'Angelo hadn't parked too close to the curb. Baseball if there were enough arms and nobody's mother needed them home before supper.

Cedarbrook was hardly a field. More a habit than a ballpark. Grass in patches. Dirt packed hard where boys had worn their turns into it. Marsh behind center swallowed anything hit clean. The backstop had been bent and patched so many times it looked held together by foul tips and argument.

It had been a field before it had been a symbol. Older men remembered chalk lines pulled across this dirt in another decade, when Fred Davis and a younger George measured bases with borrowed tape and called it a start. By 1969, weather and neglect had thinned that memory.

The ground still knew the game, but the town had stopped knowing how much it needed it.

If nobody had a real base, they used a pizza box, a sweatshirt, a piece of cardboard ripped from a carton. Everybody knew where the lines were anyway.

Down the hill, the grown-ups lived by a different clock. The GE whistle on Western Avenue reached into kitchens, garages, union coats, church clothes. Men came home with oil at the cuffs and metal still in their ears. Women set food on the table and stretched pay the way only tired people know how to stretch it.

On Sundays the houses filled up anyway. Sauce on the stove. Bread torn by hand.

Stories crossing over each other before they finished. Somebody always at the door. Somebody always staying.

Kids noticed it anyway: the way a patched field could pull a whole block toward it before supper.

Near the head of the table sat the hardest-working man in the house, Old Spice on his collar, Pall Malls on his breath. All week he worried about today and refused to talk about tomorrow. On Sundays something loosened. He'd lean back with his coffee and laugh, sometimes dropping a half-sung Elvis line into the noise.

"I'll worry about tomorrow," men like that would say, "when tomorrow becomes today."

On some nightstands, four dimes waited in a neat little row—enough for a couple of packs of baseball cards and one coin left over, set there by hands too tired to count a full pay envelope. Lucky numbers, a father might say. Four and one. April first, nineteen forty-one. That's me.

That world shaped its mentors—men and women who'd grown up in the '30s, '40s, and '50s, survived wars and layoffs and winters that froze pipes solid, and still believed the right thing to do was give something back. They weren't "development coaches" or "program directors." They were the cop who waved kids across the street, the teacher who stayed after the bell to help with long division, the diner waitress who topped off coffee and courage in the same motion. Lessons came in a firm handshake, a well-thrown grounder, a quiet ride home after a bad game.

At night, WBZ stitched those lives together—weather, ball scores, traffic along Route 1. Mill towns, row houses. And triple-deckers all listened to the same voice. Out by the highway, neon cows and restaurant signs glowed through the dark, promising steak tips, and a night where someone else did the work. It all looked permanent then.

That illusion ended one winter night when the radio changed its voice.

WBZ was low on the windowsill, half swallowed by the hiss of the kettle. Mary Davis had a dish towel over her shoulder and soap on her hands when the announcer cut into the music — flat, careful. Breaking news out of Saugus. Route 1. Red Coach Grill. Shots fired. Two officers down.

George looked up from the table where he and Fred had been counting bills into three piles. Nobody in the room moved. He reached over and turned the knob until the words came through clean. Mary set the towel down. When the phone rang, George answered with one word and listened the way men listen when the world has already decided something without asking them.

After that, the town divided the way towns do. Some people locked their doors earlier and kept their heads down. Others started looking for something that might hold. For Fred Davis, that something began with cedar posts, frozen ground, and a line by the creek.

The field was old. The fence would be new. That distinction mattered. Fred was not inventing Cedarbrook; he was trying to reclaim it before grief, fear, and profit could turn it into another forgotten patch of dirt.

Years later, boys would lean on that rail without knowing all it had cost to raise it. For now there was only a man in the cold, a hammer in his hand, and the first stretch of ground he meant to claim back for children.

That is where this story starts.

Part One — The Field and the Fire

©

(1969–1971)

Chapter One — The Creek and the Nails

©

(Winter 1970 · Saugus, Massachusetts)

ON BARROW STREET, MARY Davis, newly widowed and still measuring her mornings by Fred's absence, kept the newspaper folded to the same column, the ink smudged where her thumb had worried it all week. WBZ murmured under the kettle. When a siren climbed Route 1, she stopped stirring and listened until it faded.

Her son George came in from the back stairwell with cold in his hair and a hammer hooked in his belt. Mary slid the mason jar of nails across the table. "Take these," she said.

"And take your gloves. The ground's iron today."

He pocketed the nails one handful at a time, the metal clicking like small change. "I'll be back before dark," he said. Mary didn't answer right away. She reached for his sleeve, gave it a squeeze, and let go like she was practicing for worse.

Down by the creek behind Chestnut Street, George Davis swung a hammer into frozen ground, rhythm steady and defiant. Each strike cracked the quiet, echoing off ice-crusted banks. Breath rose in bursts.

He wasn't building for beauty. He was building because he had to.

Fred Davis—George's father, his shadow, and his conscience—had dropped on the factory floor a month earlier, his heart giving out between one shift and the next at GE. His work gloves and dented lunch pail still sat by the front hall closet, too sacred to throw out, too painful to move.

The GE whistle still blew. Route 1 still hummed. Kids still knocked on back doors, asking if anyone could come out to play.

Mary Davis watched from the kitchen window, hands wrapped around an untasted mug.

Fog blurred George's outline: shoulders hunched, body bent by exhaustion and purpose.

On the counter, the radio murmured WBZ through static.

"From docks to diner lots, you're listening to WBZ. Keep warm—it's twelve degrees along Route 1."

Mary turned the volume down. The voice sounded too calm for a world that had cracked open.

She traced the mug's chip with her thumb. Fred had given it to her before Michael's enlistment. Coffee tastes better when it remembers, he'd told her. Now it felt less like a joke and more like an unfinished prayer.

That night, George came in raw-faced and blistered. He hung his coat by the stove and stood a moment, thawing in pine-and-smoke silence. Mary poured coffee and set it beside the new ledger she had opened after Fred's funeral—not George's old field log of names, games, and borrowed summers, but her own: neat columns of names and notes, debts both financial and moral, a record of things left unsaid.

"How many posts?" she asked.

"Four," he said.

"Ground doesn't want them."

"Good," she said.

"Neither do you."

He managed half a smile.

"I'd rather it be me."

She watched him over the mug.

"You ever think the fence is too much?"

He looked at her like she'd asked him to quit on the dead.

"Fred liked things straight. So do I."

"I'm finishing what he started."

She wanted to argue—grief wasn't measured in blisters—but his calluses answered for him.

Weeks later, the creek froze solid. The sound of metal on wood carried down the banks like a heartbeat.

Parker Greene's truck began appearing in the mornings, engine idling until he shut it off and joined George at the line of posts.

Parker had held Forni that night at the Red Coach, snow going red under his knees. The guilt had never fully left him.

"You keep this up, you're going to drop right here in the mud," Parker said, stepping over the frost-bitten boards.

"Then I'll have company,"

George said.

"Cut that out."

"For him."

Parker let the hammer blows speak for a few breaths.

"Fences don't keep people out," he said finally. "They show who'll climb."

"Maybe that's the point."

"Then build it high."

Afternoon dimmed behind the Hilltop cow on Route 1, its metal silhouette watching over traffic and snow. George worked until his gloves burned, Fred's Thanksgiving words landing with each set post: Something good to hold on to, Georgie. Reminds people what honest looks like.

When his arm finally quit, he let the hammer fall into the snow.

The line stretched nearly twenty yards—crooked, but standing.

From the house, Mary's silhouette bent over her notebook. George wanted to tell her it wasn't just about grief anymore—that it was about decency, about giving people something to lean on when the world refused to slow down—but the words stayed lodged where his breath turned to steam. He picked up the hammer again.

A few days later, a thin thaw teased the air. The creek whispered under the ice. Mary met Parker outside the post office, his cigarette half-burned, cap pulled low. "How's he holding?" Parker asked.

"Better with a hammer," she said.

"He sleep?"

"Not with Da Nang on the news."

Parker looked toward the street.

"Figured."

"You were there," she said.

"Feels like a film loop," he answered.

"Somebody forgot to turn it off."

"Then do something good with it."

"That's what this is," he said, nodding toward the creek.

"Make sure it holds," she said.

That evening George came in smelling of sawdust and iron. He sat at the table; Mary poured.

"Fred used to say you can't fix people,"

George murmured, looking at his hands, "but you can give them something to lean on."

Mary nodded once.

"That sounds like him."

She laid her hand over his.

"Then build it so it stands."

His shoulders eased, just a fraction—the first time since the funeral that anything in him seemed to unclench.

The next morning, Parker showed up carrying a box of nails.

"Running short," he said.

George smiled.

"Appreciate it."

"Did Fred ever tell you what he really wanted this fence for?" Parker asked.

"To keep kids out of the creek,"

George said.

"That's what he told people."

George frowned.

"What'd he tell you?"

Parker looked past him at the posts. "He told me a place goes bad when nobody bothers to mark the edge."

George studied the half-healed blisters across his palms. "He was right."

By sundown, snow fell heavy, whitening the new rails. George's last swing rang. For a moment, Mary thought she heard Fred laugh on the wind. Soft. Impossible. Enough to steady her.

She opened the ledger.

Entry #1—Fence started. Ground hard. Line holding.

She let the ink dry, then looked out at the posts cutting through the snow.

A car passed on Route 1, WBZ trailing thin through the dark.

Mary touched the cold glass and said, this time to no one but herself, "Good. Let it hold."

Chapter Two — Mrs. Foster's Mornings

©

(Early Spring 1971 · Lynn–Saugus Line)

BY THE TIME THE first thaw reached Chestnut Street, winter had loosened its grip but not its ghosts. The gray banks along the curbs shrank back, leaving what the season hadn't bothered to keep—salt cans, cigarette filters, a crumpled Red Sox scorecard from last October.

The air carried its usual morning mix: yeast from the bakery, exhaust from the buses, a chemical note drifting up from Route 107. Around here, that smell was as close to a clock as anyone needed.

Inside Mrs. Foster's Donuts, steam filmed the windows and turned the street into soft shapes—headlights, a church steeple, the suggestion of the Lynn marsh road if you knew where to look.

The sign out front had been there as long as anyone could remember:

MRS. FOSTER'S DONUTS · COFFEE SINCE 1955

The paint had chipped at the corners, not enough to look tired, just enough to look honest. Mrs. Foster herself had stepped back the year before, eyes not what they'd been. But no one would let the name come down. The Delios family ran it now, cousins to the Kane's crew over on Lincoln Avenue. Peter stayed in the back with the fryer, humming Sinatra against the hiss of oil. Kay held the counter with a dancer's balance and a mother's memory for orders.

She didn't need a pad.

"Two jellies, one cruller, black with six," she said as a man in a navy pea coat dropped onto a stool.

"That's creepy, Kay," he said, though his hand was already reaching for the sugar. "It's habit," she replied.

"You're the one who never changes."

Along the front window, a row of stools held the usual morning council: three retirees in wool caps, a mailman half in uniform. And a machinist named Eddie who came straight off third shift at GE, hands still smelling of metal and solvent. Their talk rolled along in a low, steady current until a single word sharpened it.

"Red Coach."

"Belmonte."

"Forni."

The names still had weight. They didn't say much about that night—just enough so no one forgot it had been real. Cups clicked against saucers; spoons stirred sugar through thick, brown coffee. Every so often, someone glanced at the door out of habit, as if expecting a patrolman to step in and shake the March cold from his coat.

Mary Davis pushed the door open just after seven, the bell giving a brighter ring for her than for anyone else. She stamped the slush from her boots and slipped her gloves into her coat pocket, pausing until her eyes adjusted from the gray outside to the yellow warmth inside.

"Morning, Mrs. Davis," Kay called.

"You look like you walked through the whole winter to get here."

"Feels like I did,"

Mary said, unbuttoning her coat. "Six plain, six glazed. And a coffee—milk, no sugar."

Kay was already reaching for the waxed box. "George out with his hammer again?"

"He'd sleep with it if I let him,"

Mary said.

"Fence doesn't build itself."

Eddie at the counter snorted. "From what I hear, that fence is half done and twice as famous as the town hall."

"That fence," one of the old men said, "is the only thing around here that's straight anymore."

The others chuckled, but the line landed like truth.

Mary slid onto an empty stool while Kay filled the box.

Smell wrapped around her—fresh dough, burnt coffee, wet wool, Old Spice, the citron bite of dish soap. For a moment, it felt like the Sundays of her childhood: crowded tables, ashtrays and laughter, people drifting in and out of the house until long after dark. Then she remembered why the town clung so tightly to its routines. Routines kept your mind from circling the things you couldn't fix.

"You holding up, hon?" Kay asked, leaning on one elbow so the question didn't carry.

"Some days better than others,"

Mary answered.

"Today's a 'one foot in front of the other' day."

Kay nodded. "Well, you tell that husband of yours the coffee's paid for as long as that fence keeps going up."

"He'd rather pay,"

Mary said.

"Feels funny taking anything free these days."

"Then don't tell him. I'll just 'forget' to ring you in."

The bell chimed again. Parker Greene walked in with his cap low, jacket zipped a little too high for the mild air. He stomped his boots and scanned the room before taking the last open stool near the end.

"Morning," he said to the counter at large.

A murmur of "Morning, Parker" rolled back.

Kay reached for another mug. "Let me guess—black, no sugar, and whatever's left in the tray?"

"Dealer's choice," he said.

"As long as it's real and not from a box."

"You wound me,"

Peter called from the back. "These hands don't make box donuts."

Parker managed half a smile, then noticed Mary. "How's George?" he asked.

"Stubborn."

She wrapped her hands around her cup. "Which is the same thing as 'still breathing' in that house."

"He was out there before dawn,"

Parker said.

"Drove by the creek on my way in.

Thought I heard church bells. Turns out it was just his hammer."

"That's the idea," Mary said.

For a moment, all three of them let that sit. The fryer sizzled. Sinatra drifted through the wall—"Fly Me to the Moon" caught somewhere around the second verse.

At the window, the retirees had drifted back to their version of news.

"They say Winter Hill's been sniffing around the Route 1 money," one said, tapping ash into his saucer.

"Winter Hill's been sniffing around everything," another replied.

"Doesn't mean they get to take it."

"Refinery men will be back," the third added.

"Men like that don't hear 'no' the first time."

Mary listened without turning her head. The words slid into her like cold water. Route 1. Winter Hill. Refinery. Names that meant her world might change again whether it wanted to or not.

Kay saw the way Mary's shoulders tightened and shifted the subject with the ease of someone who'd been running mornings long enough to steer whole towns.

"Red Sox will be better this year," she said to the room. "Mark my words."

"Mary's the baseball prophet,"

Eddie said.

"That Thompson boy's got an arm like a whip."

"Jack's twelve,"

Mary said.

"He's got chores like everyone else."

"Still,"

Eddie replied, "kid throws like he's older."

Mary pictured Jack in the backyard, a sock pulled over a ball so he wouldn't break the fence boards George hadn't meant for batting practice. She thought of the times he'd thrown to no one, talking under his breath like he was calling his own game. The town needed something to look forward to. Boys' arms had always done that job.

Kay slid the donut box toward her across the counter. "Six and six," she said.

"Tell Jack to come by when school lets out. I'll sneak him a cruller if he brings me a box score."

"He'll hold you to that," Mary said, tucking the box under her arm. As she reached for her gloves, she felt the edge of the ledger in her bag, corners worn soft from the past months. Names, numbers, notes—things owed and things forgiven. For a heartbeat she considered taking it out right there, setting it on the counter like a challenge.

Instead, she left it where it was. There would be time enough for ink and courage. For now, the town needed coffee and a place to sit where the world still made some kind of sense.

Outside, thaw dripped from the eaves in slow beads. Across the street, a school bus groaned to a stop, doors wheezing open, kids yelling over each other as they climbed aboard. Life, uncaring, continued at full volume.

Mary stepped into the chill, donut box warm against her coat. From this angle she could see a sliver of the creek road if she squinted past the roofs. She imagined George out there already, hammer ringing against damp wood, building something straight in a crooked season.

She took a breath that tasted like yeast, exhaust, and the last edge of winter.

"Coffee, gossip, grief," she murmured.

"Whole town runs on it."

Then she started up the street toward home, following the smell of sawdust and the faint, steady echo of work somewhere beyond the trees.

Chapter Three — The Fence in Winter

©

(Winter 1971 · Saugus, Massachusetts)

BY THE FIRST SNOW of 1971, the fence along the creek had become more than cedar and nails.

To most in town, it was Fred's fence—a line drawn against forgetting. Kids who rode their bikes past it slowed without knowing why. Men in pickup trucks tipped their caps as they rolled by, a small, private salute to what it represented.

The papers had stopped writing about the Red Coach Grill, but people hadn't stopped remembering. The sign still flickered out front, red neon humming against the cold. On windy nights, if you were quiet, you could almost hear sirens stitched into the dark—a sound the town carried in its bones.

George Davis worked the fence through it all. The rhythm of nail and rail kept him upright even as his joints ached and his breath shortened. He'd been out there so long he could tell the hour by the light on the boards. Mornings turned them silver. Afternoons washed them blue. At dusk, they caught the color of a dying sun, warm as memory.

Every morning, Mary packed his thermos and wrapped his scarf twice. Every night, she boiled water for his hands and rubbed warmth back into his knuckles until he stopped wincing. He never complained. But she could tell—by the way he set the tools down slower, by the pauses between strikes, by how often he looked at the creek instead of the fence.

That winter, the ground froze deeper than anyone could remember.

Even the creek seemed to hold its breath.

One January morning, Parker Greene pulled up in his truck, headlights slicing through fog. He climbed out bundled in two coats, breath smoking in the cold.

"You're out here early," he said.

"Fence doesn't build itself," George replied, driving a nail home. Parker watched for a while, hands jammed in his pockets.

"You ever gonna tell her you can't feel your fingers?"

"She already knows,"

George said.

"Pretends she doesn't so I'll keep pretending I can."

Parker crouched and picked up a board. "Brought a few extras from the yard. Good lumber. Thicker grain, less rot."

"Appreciate it."

"You ever think about resting?"

"Resting's for after."

"After what?"

Another nail set. The sound cracked the morning. "After it's done."

In town, refinery talk grew heavier—less if and more when.

At Mrs. Foster's, at the barber, at the GE gates, conversations slid from the Red Sox to "Hartwell's offer" and what it might mean for taxes, for jobs, for the marsh. No one said aloud what it might mean for the creek and the field, but everybody thought it.

Mary heard it all in fragments—whispers over coffee, clippings slid across counters, a line here or there from Parker when he came by for supper. She tucked every piece away, the way she tucked grocery receipts and school notices into her ledger: proof that something had happened, even if you couldn't yet see where it was leading.

George's cough deepened. He ignored it the way men like him ignored everything that didn't bleed. "You sound worse," Mary said one night as he pulled off his boots.

"Just the cold sitting on my chest," he answered.

She didn't argue. She made an appointment and told him only when it was time to go.

The doctor listened to his lungs, frowned, and told him to take it easy. Pneumonia if he wasn't careful. George nodded in all the right places, then spent the drive home staring out the window at bare trees and telephone wires.

"How long you think he's been breathing like that?" the doctor asked Mary quietly in the hall. "Since Fred died," she said.

That night she sat George by the stove and wrapped his hands in towels warmed in boiling water.

"You're burning yourself down," she said.

"Not yet," he answered.

"Your hands say different."

He looked down. His palms were a map of scars and calluses. "Every one of those is a promise."

"Fred wouldn't want you breaking yourself for his memory,"

Mary said.

"That's exactly what he'd want."

She sighed, finished rubbing his wrists, and kissed his knuckles. "Then at least let me share the weight."

He nodded, though they both knew he wouldn't.

Outside, the fence stood half buried in snow, rails capped with white. Under the streetlights, each post cast a long shadow across the field.

Kids started calling it The Line.

Jack Thompson, Anthony's boy from three houses down, had started showing up at the fence whether there was a game or not.

When the first thaw came in March, they returned to the creek, tossing stones across the melting ice and daring each other to climb the lowest rails. Jack and his friends measured themselves against the posts—backs pressed to wood, heels dug into mud, checking how high their heads reached on cedar that didn't move.

"Someday I'll be taller than this one," Jack said, patting a middle post.

Parker, carrying a bundle of new boards, heard him. "Fence will still be here," he said.

"That's the idea."

Spring edged in on small signs: a trickle of water under the ice, the first brave patch of brown grass along the third-base line, the way dusk arrived a few minutes later each night. George worked through it all, slower now, taking more breaks, refusing to let a day pass without setting at least one nail.

At the kitchen table, Mary opened her ledger and ran her fingers over the first entry.

Entry #1—When the world breaks, start with what you can hold.

She added another, ink catching the light.

Entry #12—If the fence holds, maybe we do too.

She closed the book and let her hand rest on the cover. The thought scared her with how much she believed it.

One rainy afternoon, Parker came in for coffee, shrugging off his jacket by the door. George sat at the table with the ledger open, tracing the column of names as if they were knotholes in a board.

"Didn't know you were the bookkeeper,"

Parker said.

"I'm not,"

George replied.

"Just checking what I owe."

Mary slid the ledger away before he could read the entries. "You're paid up," she said.

"Doesn't feel that way,"

George answered. Parker pulled out a chair. "Fence says otherwise."

George stared at him. "You got a way with words for a man who barely talks."

"Comes from listening,"

Parker said.

"You hear enough weak promises, you start craving the strong ones."

Later that week, George drove the last nail into the last rail. The sound ran down the creek and out toward the marsh, a clear, final note.

Mary joined him and took his arm.

"It's beautiful," she said.

"Straight enough?"

"Straight enough to hold."

That night, WBZ's sign-off drifted across the living room, soft through the static, without the full flourish they sometimes gave it:

"...from the mills to the marshes, from Fenway to fences that keep a town together—you're listening to WBZ."

Mary turned to George. "They're talking about us again." He closed his eyes, smiling.

"Maybe they always were."

Chapter Four — Letters from Da Nang

©

(1967–1968 · Saugus, Massachusetts / Da Nang, Vietnam)

MICHAEL'S LETTERS CAME IN bunches. Some weeks, nothing. Then three envelopes at once, rubber band biting into the paper, his name in a hand that still looked like the boy who'd written book reports at the kitchen table.

The first letters were almost light.

Dear Ma and Dad,

Da Nang's hotter than any July we ever had, but they say you get used to it. We both know they lie, so don't worry if I sweat right through this paper. Food's not Sunday dinner, but it's food. They've got a guy here from Worcester who swears he can make decent sauce out of the mess hall tomatoes. I told him he's never met you.

Tell Jack I saw a kid throw today with his arm all over the place.

Made me miss him throwing into the side of the house.

Love, Michael

Mary read that one three times before George came home, smoothing the edges flat against the table. Steam from the kettle fogged the edges of the words.

"He sounds like himself," she said as George sat down. "He's trying to,"

George answered.

They didn't say what they were both thinking—that if Michael was making jokes about sauce, he was still far enough from the worst of it.

The next letter talked about a pickup game on a strip of packed dirt behind the barracks.

We don't have real bases, so we use whatever's not nailed down—helmets, ammo crates, a crate of peaches somebody "borrowed." You should've seen the look on the sergeant's face when he realized "third base" had disappeared.

I played short. Don't tell Jack I booted one.

Tell him the fence better be ready when I get home. I want to see if I can still hit it.

Mary smiled at that, even as her hand tightened on the page. The fence had become the way Michael measured time now—before it, after it, and what he'd do when he came back to it.

As the months rolled, the tone shifted. Jokes thinned. More lines fell into the spaces between what he said and what he didn't.

Dear Ma,

You don't hear the crickets here. Just generators and choppers and guys trying not to cough. The air smells like smoke even on clear days.

We pulled a double shift last week. I'm fine, just tired. The nights are longer than they should be.

Tell Dad not to worry. I remember everything he told me about keeping my head and watching my corners.

Tell Jack to keep throwing. I'll need a catcher when I get back.

Love you,

Michael

Mary read that one standing at the sink, dishwater cooling around her wrists. For a moment she couldn't move, the lines blurring until the ink looked like it might slide right off the page.

In the next room, Jack sat at the table with his math book open, pencil hovering above the same problem he'd been staring at for ten minutes.

"Is it bad?" he asked without turning around.

"It's a letter from Michael,"

Mary said.

"He's tired. He's okay."

Jack nodded slowly. "Okay like he says, or okay like you say?"

She considered lying, then didn't. "Okay like he says, for now."

George read that letter with his jaw set, thumb pressed into the fold until the paper creased.

"He's working too hard," he said.

"That's what you hear?"

Mary asked.

"I hear a man doing his job,"

George replied.

"I hear someone who needs a decent night's sleep."

Mary wanted to tell him she heard the muffled edge of fear in every sentence, but she knew better. Some truths you didn't push on a man who was building a fence to stay upright.

Another letter came in midwinter, the envelope damp at the corners.

Dear Ma and Dad,

They don't always let us say what's going on, so if I sound like I'm writing in circles, it's because I am. The other night the sky went from blue to orange to nothing in about ten seconds. You could feel the heat through your boots. Afterwards it smelled like somebody lit a tire fire and forgot how to put it out. We're all here. That's the important part.

Some nights I shut my eyes and build WBZ out of static. I tell myself the crackle is just the set fighting for Boston and not this place trying to swallow every familiar sound.

Tell Jack to throw one for me at the field. Just one. Right down the middle. Love,

Michael

Mary didn't cry when she read that one. The fear had climbed past tears into something harder. She folded the letter carefully and slid it into the drawer where she kept insurance papers and birth certificates and the recipe her mother had written for Sunday sauce. Things you didn't throw away.

Later, when the house was quiet, she took out the ledger.

Entry #19—Letters can lie on the surface and still tell the truth underneath.

She thought of adding more—that every line Michael didn't write said as much as the ones he did—but closed the book instead.

George began to read the return address on the envelopes before he broke the seal. He named the base out loud, a small ritual that seemed to keep it where it belonged.

"Da Nang," he'd say, the words flat and careful. "He's still in Da Nang."

One night, a different color envelope came—a thin blue aerogramme, edges worn. Mary knew before she unfolded it that this one was going to live in a different place in her memory.

Dear Ma,

This one might get clipped by the censors, so I'll keep it short.

We lost a boy from Everett last week. He was here and then he wasn't, and that's as much as they'll let me say. I didn't know him well, but he had a laugh that sounded like he couldn't believe he'd ended up this far from home.

It made me think about all the kids back there who think time is guaranteed. Please make sure Jack knows it isn't. Not in a scary way. Just... real.

If you don't hear from me for a bit, it's not because something's wrong. It's because things are loud. I love you. Tell Dad I hear the fence in my head when I try to sleep.

Michael

Mary read that one at the table, elbows planted, hands shaking just enough that the page rustled. When she looked up, George was already watching her.

"Different?" he asked.

She swallowed. "Different."

He took the letter and read it once. His eyes didn't leave the page, but his hand reached blindly across the table until it found hers.

In the weeks that followed, fewer letters came. When they did, they seemed to land heavier on the kitchen table, as if carrying the weight of all the unsent ones. The words themselves grew simpler.

I'm here. I'm working.

Tell Jack I'm proud of him.

Mary started reading them aloud to the fence. On days when George worked past sundown, she would walk down to the creek, stand with her gloved hands on the top rail, and whisper the lines into the cold.

"Michael hears you," she told Jack when he caught her once, eyes wide.

"How?"

"Same way we hear him," she said.

"Whether the letters show up or not."

Jack put his palm flat on the rough wood. For the first time, he understood that the fence wasn't just about keeping kids from the water or keeping memories in one place. It was a kind of reply—a straight line laid down in answer to a world that kept sending crooked news.

Up in their bedroom that night, Mary slid the newest letter into the drawer with the others. The stack had grown thick enough to tilt.

She rested her hand on it a moment longer than usual.

If the fence holds, maybe we do too, she thought, and shut the drawer before the thought could scare her. Months later, when the letters stopped and the knock finally came at the front door, she would tuck that blue aerogramme on top of the others. The Gold Star in the Davis window would say what the pages no longer could.

Outside, wind scraped along the boards. Somewhere high above the clouds, planes moved east and west, carrying boys who would write home and boys who never would.

Down in Saugus, the fence along the creek stood straight in the winter dark, waiting to see which kind of letter would come next.

Part Two — The Flood and the Fight

©

(1972–1975)

Chapter Five — Hartwell's Offer

©

(Late Spring 1973 · Saugus Town Line)

BY THE TIME THE lilacs bloomed along Route 1, Saugus was holding its breath again.

The refinery proposal—quiet for months—had come back under a new name: Providence Development Partners.

Same suits. Same trucks. Different letterhead.

From the kitchen window, Mary Davis saw the first sign. New survey flags—orange instead of red—fluttered along the reeds near the creek, bright against the pale green. Fresh stakes had been driven sometime between night and dawn, thin splinters of someone else's plans.

"George," she called, wiping her hands on a dish towel. "You see this?"

He stepped out onto the porch, hammer already on his belt. The boards he'd put up that winter had weathered to a soft gray. They looked like they'd been there forever.

He followed her gaze.

"Thought we sent them packing," he said.

"Thought wrong," Mary replied.

Down by the water, three men in hard hats and clean boots consulted a map, each pretending the fence wasn't in the way. One pointed past the posts toward the marsh, tracing a route with his finger.

"The lines run right up to the edge of Fred's fence,"

George muttered. "Not through it,"

Mary said.

One of the men glanced up, saw them watching, and looked away too quickly.

At Mrs. Foster's, the air smelled like coffee and nerves.

Kay slid a mug toward Parker Greene and topped it off without asking.

"Thought this was over," he said, nodding toward the window where a Providence truck idled at the corner.

"Men like that don't understand over,"

Kay said.

"They understand done. And we're not done yet."

On the front stools, the retirees read the paper, lips moving silently over the same headlines: INDUSTRIAL ZONING REVISITED

REFINERY PLAN BACK ON TABLE

"They're saying new name, new jobs, new money," one of them snorted. "Same old smoke."

Mary slipped into the seat beside Parker.

"Flags are back at the creek," she said.

"I saw," he answered.

"They've been knocking on doors near the marsh.

Saying words like

'opportunity' and 'partnership.'"

"Partnership for who?"

Mary asked.

"For whoever signs first,"

Parker said.

"For everyone else, it's exhaust."

He took a long drink, then set the mug down a little too hard. "Hartwell's behind it," he added.

"Same boys, different banner.

Town Hall sweetheart. Councilman of the Year. Man's a handshake with a knife in it."

Mary frowned. "You sure?"

Parker gave her a look. "I know a man who wants a cut when I see one."

Kay leaned closer. "He was in here last week. Talking about 'unlocking the potential of underutilized land.' "

" 'Underutilized land,' "

Mary repeated. "That what we're calling kids' fields now?"

Parker shrugged. "To men like Hartwell, marsh is just profit waiting for concrete.

Kids are just noise between tax bills."

Mary's jaw tightened. "Not if I have anything to say about it."

"You planning on saying it?"

Parker asked.

Mary glanced toward the back wall, where a notice had been tacked up, slightly crooked:

PUBLIC HEARING—REVISED INDUSTRIAL ZONING PETITION 73-A

TOWN HALL, THURSDAY, 7:00 P.M.

"I am now," she said.

Town Hall smelled like old paper and cold coffee the night of the hearing. Folding chairs creaked under winter coats. The fluorescent lights buzzed overhead, bright enough to make everyone look a little more tired than usual.

Mary sat between George and Parker, petition flyers folded neatly in her lap. Around them, neighbors whispered, craning to see who had shown up and which side they were on.

Hartwell stood near the front, suit perfect, smile soft and practiced. When the council chair nodded to him, he stepped to the microphone like he'd been rehearsing the move for years.

"We're here tonight to talk about progress," he began. "About responsible growth.

About unlocking the potential of land that, frankly, has been sitting idle for too long."

He gestured toward a map on an easel—lines and blocks in colors that meant more to surveyors than to the people sitting under them.

"The Providence project," he went on, "brings tax relief, jobs, infrastructure improvements. It's a partnership between business and community."

Mary heard the words and thought of men in clean boots staring past her fence.

A Providence representative followed—Collins, according to his name tag.

He spoke the same language: revenue, stability, modern facilities, regional competitiveness. The phrases blended into one long, polished argument that never once mentioned kids, lungs, or the way the sun set over Cedarbrook's left field.

When it was time for public comment, Parker leaned over. "Want me to go first?" he asked.

Mary shook her head. "No. They need to hear a mother before they hear a cop."

She stood, walked to the microphone, and set her hands on either side of it to keep them steady.

"My name is Mary Davis," she said.

"My family lives on Chestnut Street. My husband built the fence you can see on that map, though I notice it's missing from your lines." A few heads turned toward the map.

"I understand taxes and jobs,"

Mary continued.

"I understand budgets and 'underutilized land.' But my son learned to run on that field. He learned what it means to be out and still be safe. That marsh you call idle is where our town breathes."

Hartwell's mouth tightened just enough to show he'd heard her. "We're not against work,"

Mary said.

"We're against being the only ones asked to live downwind of someone else's paycheck."

She stepped back to a ripple of quiet applause. It wasn't a wave, but it was something.

They didn't have to wait long for the first knock.

It came two evenings later, just as Jack was finishing his homework and the news began its slow roll through oil prices, Sox scores, and trouble in places the Davises would never see.

George opened the door to a man in a neat sport coat, hair parted as carefully as his sentences.

"Mr. Davis," he said, extending a hand. "I'm with Providence Development Partners. My name's Collins. We're—"

"Here about the creek," George said.

The man smiled. "Here about opportunities, yes. For all of Saugus."

He talked about tax revenue and jobs, about keeping up with the times, about being "part of the future instead of standing in its way." Words like partnership, growth, and security fell from his mouth like coins from a machine.

"You're right on the edge of the proposed improvement zone," he said.

"Prime location. Providence believes in fair compensation for affected landowners. We can offer—"

"This isn't 'affected land,' "

George cut in. "This is where my kid plays ball."

Collins glanced past him at the fence line. His eyes skimmed the boards like they were in the way of a project, not the center of a life.

"I understand your attachment," he said smoothly. "But sometimes we have to make hard choices for the greater good."

"You understand nothing," Mary said from the doorway behind George, ledger tucked under her arm.

"Especially not the cost of someone else's good."

"Mrs. Davis,"

Collins replied, "we're talking about substantial benefits for the community. Scholarships, roadwork, school support. Longterm security. Don't you want that for your son?"

"He already has something long-term,"

Mary said.

"It's called a childhood."

George stepped fully into the doorway, blocking the view. "We're not interested," he said.

"Think it over,"

Collins replied, smile never quite reaching his eyes. "The council will be voting. It's better to be with progress than against it."

Parker's words echoed in George's head: a handshake with a knife in it.

"Progress doesn't mean tearing down what's holding things together," George said. He closed the door.

Later that night, Parker stopped by, knocking his boots against the porch to shake off the day.

"He come?" he asked, stepping inside. "Him or one just like him,"

George said.

"They'll keep coming,"

Parker said.

"Men like that don't hear 'no.' They hear 'try harder.' "

"What else did your friend say?"

Mary asked. Parker took off his cap, turned it in his hands.

"Word is Providence has been promising more than wages," he said.

"Talking to some boys north of

Boston. Men with mirrors for eyes. They don't care whose field it is as long as they get paid."

"Winter Hill," George said quietly.

Parker nodded once. "Hartwell gets his refinery, they get a slice.

That's the rumor."

Mary pressed her pen harder than she meant to. The nib dug a groove into the paper of her ledger.

"We'll be ready," she said.

She turned to a clean line and wrote:

Entry #27—When men threaten your peace, build louder. When they try to buy your silence, write louder.

She closed the book and looked at both men.

"They're counting on people being tired," she said.

"We don't get to be tired yet."

Down by the creek, the new survey flags snapped in the evening breeze. The fence didn't move.

(Late Spring 1972 · Town Hall Basement)

Mary had not planned to go back into Town Hall that week.

But the library's heat had broken again and Mrs. Foster had called, voice tight, to say the boys were "making a clubhouse out of the history stacks" and that if Mary didn't come down, the librarian was going to.

Mary came with a paper bag of peanut butter sandwiches and the tired patience of a woman who'd learned that boys do not respond to lectures as well as they respond to lunch.

The Town Hall basement smelled like old paint and damp paper. Someone had pinned election flyers to the bulletin board until the board had given up and sagged. A box fan rattled in the corner, pushing warm air in lazy circles.

The boys were not in the history stacks.

They were outside the clerk's office, where the door stood half open and a man's voice carried out into the hall.

"—there's the creek line," the man was saying. "And here's the fence. That's the problem. It looks innocent. It's not."

Mary slowed. She shifted the sandwiches to her left arm. Her right hand found the strap of her bag.

Inside, two men leaned over a table. The first wore a sports coat that was too crisp for Cedarbrook. The second wore a gray work shirt with a name patch stitched over the pocket: COLLINS. He held a pencil like a weapon, tapping it on a map that had been unrolled across the table.

On the map, the creek was a thin blue line. The fence was a darker one, drawn with the confidence of someone who believed paper outranked wood.

At the edge of the table, Parker stood with his hands in his pockets. Mary felt her stomach tighten. Parker's presence in a room always meant somebody had decided something before the rest of the town arrived.

Collins angled the pencil. "The surveyors can flag it by Friday," he said.

"We'll make it clean. Legal. Like it was always meant to be."

The man in the sports coat smiled without warmth. "Hartwell wants no drama," he said.

"We don't do drama. We do process. Process is polite."

Parker's jaw flexed. "And if the Davises don't cooperate?"

The sports coat man didn't look up from the map. "Then you'll do what you're already doing," he said lightly, as if Parker were a service. "You'll remind them about permits. Access. Liability. You'll remind them that fences can be moved."

Collins chuckled. "Or burned," he muttered, then caught himself and cleared his throat like a man who'd said the quiet part out loud. Parker's eyes flicked up. For a moment, he looked older than he was, like he could already see the headline somebody would pretend to regret.

Mary's fingers went cold.

The sports coat man slid a folder across the table. The tab on the front read: DAVIS, GEORGE. Under it, in neat type, was another word: EASEMENT.

"Here," the man said.

"This is the original utility access clause. Most people don't read it. Most people don't understand it. But it gives us enough room. We don't need to take the field. We just need to take the story."

Parker stared at the folder. "They built that fence," he said. It wasn't a protest. It was a statement of fact, the kind facts used to be.

"And we can unbuild it," the man replied.

"With paperwork first.

With pressure second. With enforcement third." Outside the door, Mary's breath caught.

One of the boys behind her—Eddie, she realized, by the restless shift of his weight—whispered, "That's my dad's name," and she understood he'd read the folder too fast, catching only the idea of a file with the power to swallow people.

Mary leaned back so the men inside would not see her shadow.

She should leave. She should not know this. Knowing things in Cedarbrook was dangerous; it made you responsible.

But the map on the table was the field she'd watched her husband build with his hands. The blue line was the creek where boys rinsed blood off scraped knees and pretended it was nothing. The dark line was the fence, and the fence was not a line. It was a promise, hammered into winter.

Mary stepped away from the door, silent as a woman who'd spent her life learning how to move through men's plans.

She walked down the basement stairs without running.

At the bottom, she stopped and opened her bag. Her ledger was there, wrapped in a dish towel like it deserved protection.

She took it out and found a fresh line.

Entry #28—They have a map. They have a folder. They have a word for taking what isn't theirs.

She paused, pencil hovering.

Entry #28—We have the fence. We have the kids. We have the truth.

Above her, in the clerk's office, a pen scratched against paper.

Mary underlined truth once, then closed the book. When she looked up, Eddie was watching her with the same expression he wore when he waited for a pitch: wary, ready, afraid of hope.

"Come on," she said, holding out the sandwiches. "You're not eating in a basement like you're already a ghost."

They followed her out into the daylight, and as Mary pushed open the Town Hall door, she could feel the weight of that folder in the room behind her like a threat with a name.

Down by the creek, the survey flags snapped in the evening breeze.

Mary did not wave back.

(That Night · Hartwell Regional Office · Route 1 Corridor)

Carver kept the blinds half-drawn, not because there was anything to hide from Route 1, but because he liked the feeling of deciding what light got in.

He stood at the window anyway, tie loosened, the town laid out below as a scatter of sodium lamps and small stubborn houses. On his desk sat a folder labeled SAUGUS—DUE DILIGENCE in block letters that looked like they belonged on a courtroom exhibit.

Collins dropped into the chair opposite him and rolled his shoulders. His hands still smelled faintly of cedar from the stakes they had planted that afternoon.

"She is not scared,"

Collins said.

"Davis's wife. The one with the ledger."

Carver did not turn. "She does not have to be scared," he replied.

"She has to be made responsible."

Collins gave a short laugh. "Responsible for what? Kids playing ball?"

Carver finally faced him. His smile was professional, practiced. "For the moment when a child gets hurt," he said. "For the moment an ambulance arrives. For the moment a reporter asks why the town allowed an unpermitted field to operate after warnings.

People do not remember who hammered the fence. They remember whose signature is on the minutes."

Collins leaned forward. "Parker is not clean in this."

"No one is clean in a small town, Collins. That is why small towns are easy to manage."

Carver tapped the folder. "Parker is already building an incident file. All we do is give him reasons."

"And the petition?" Collins asked.

Carver opened a second folder—thinner, and that was the point. "We do not have to beat the petition," he said.

"We have to change what it means. Tonight it means refinery. Tomorrow it means safety. Liability. Children's blood on someone else's hands."

He slid a photograph across the desk.

A grainy Polaroid, halfdeveloped, the white edge still too bright. Boys in the dark. A fence line. A light rigging that did not belong.

"After hours,"

Carver said softly. "You get me three more of these, and I can make a town afraid of its own childhood."

Collins stared at the photo a beat too long. "You are going to use kids."

"I am going to use parents,"

Carver corrected. "Kids are just what parents are willing to burn the town for."

He pulled a legal pad from beneath the folder and wrote a name: KANE. "Find the brother," he said.

"Offer him work. Offer him relief. Then offer him the chance to say, on record, that Mary Davis is risking children."

Collins stood, the chair legs scraping. "And if he will not?"

"Then you find someone who will,"

Carver said, voice still calm. "The trick is always the same: make the betrayal feel like survival."

Chapter Six — Survey Stakes

©

(Spring 1974 · The Creek)

AT SUNRISE, THE CREEK looked harmless—thin ice at the edges, cattails bent like tired wrists, the water moving with the quiet confidence of something that had outlasted every argument in town.

A truck with a Providence Development Partners logo rolled down Barrow Street like it owned the road. It stopped where the asphalt gave up and the dirt path began, and two men climbed out in canvas jackets that were too clean for mud season. One carried a tripod. One carried a clipboard. Neither carried a shovel.

George Davis watched from the fence line with his hands in his pockets and his jaw set in a way Mary recognized. It was the same set he wore when the factory foreman announced overtime like a gift, or when the bank teller said the word 'processing' as if it were a prayer.

Jack stood a few steps behind him, half-hidden by the posts. He had his glove on out of habit, because the field was where you wore your glove the way you wore your name.

The man with the clipboard smiled first, like smiling could make the rest of it polite. "Morning, Mr. Davis," he said.

"We spoke the other night. Collins."

"You brought friends," George replied.

"Surveyors,"

Collins said. He said it the way people said "doctors." Like you should stand aside and be grateful. "We have authorization to mark the perimeter of the improvement zone. Just preliminary. Just so everyone has a clear picture."

George looked past him, down the creek where the grass thinned and the marsh began. A third man was already walking, pushing a thin metal stake into the ground and tying a bright ribbon to it. The ribbon snapped once in the wind—cheerful, shameless.

Mary came out onto the back porch with her coffee still steaming. The ledger was tucked under her arm the way some women carried a Bible. She didn't call out.

Calling out made it a scene. She let it be what it already was: an invasion conducted in daylight.

George took one step forward. "That fence is the line," he said.

"That is the perimeter. You want a clear picture, look at it."

Collins kept smiling, but the smile tightened at the corners. "We respect what you've built," he said, and the word "built" sounded like a compliment and an insult at the same time. "But the line on your fence isn't the line on our map. There's a process."

"There's always a process,"

Mary said, voice carrying just enough to make the men turn. She walked down to them slowly, not hurrying, not hesitating. "There's a process for moving families. A process for closing mills. A process for turning a marsh into a smokestack."

Collins blinked. He hadn't expected the fence to come with a woman attached. "Mrs. Davis," he said.

"This isn't personal."

Mary stopped beside George. Their shoulders didn't touch, but Jack saw the way their bodies angled toward each other anyway. "It becomes personal," she said, "the moment you put a stake in a child's running path."

One of the surveyors called out from farther down the creek. "Hey, Collins—where do you want the next flag?"

(Night · Cedarbrook Field)

By nightfall, the ribbons had become a kind of insult.

In daylight they looked official, almost harmless—a neat line of pink and orange fluttering in the breeze. But at night, under the borrowed lamps Krantz rolled down on a whim, the ribbons looked like tongues.

Jack came first. He always came first when something felt wrong. He moved through the grass carefully, shoes quiet, eyes sharp.

Eddie came next, carrying a flashlight with the battery half dead. The beam wobbled over the infield dirt, then settled on the nearest stake.

The wooden peg was new. Fresh-split. It had been driven into ground that still held frost down deep.

"Like a grave marker," Eddie said, and his voice tried to make it a joke. It failed.

Ana arrived without announcing herself. She stepped out of the dark near the fence line, hands in her jacket pockets, face steady.

"Don't touch it," she said.

Jack's hand froze an inch from the stake. "We have to do something."

Ana tilted her head. "Do you know what happens when you do something to a thing that belongs to men with clipboards?" she asked.

"They don't call it self-defense. They call it damage."

Eddie kicked a clump of dirt. "So we just let them plant their little sticks like they own it?"

"No,"

Ana said.

"We remember it."

She pulled a pencil from her pocket—not a pen, a pencil, like Mary's—and in the beam of Eddie's light she scraped a small mark into the side of the stake. A tiny notch, barely visible. Then another, lower.

"What is that?" Jack asked.

"A way of saying we saw you,"

Ana replied.

"A way of saying you don't get to do this in secret."

The flashlight beam shook as Eddie's hand trembled. "My dad signed something today," he blurted. "At the mill. Parker's form. He said it was just a form."

Jack looked at him. "Did he say why?"

Eddie swallowed. "He said keeping food in the house is its own kind of fence."

The words landed hard. Jack felt them in his ribs. He had always thought fences were built by love. He had not considered they might also be built by fear.

A car door shut somewhere up the road. The sound carried clean in the cold. Ana's head snapped up.

The headlights came next, sliding along the trees, then stopping.

A truck idled on Chestnut Street, engine low, patient. The lights were not pointed at the field—not quite. They were aimed at the fence, like a reminder.

Jack's throat went dry. "We should go."

Eddie didn't move. His chin lifted, stubborn in the way boys use when they're afraid. "Why do they get to watch?" he said.

"Why do we have to hide?"

Ana didn't answer. She stepped toward the fence and laid her palm against the chain links. The metal was cold enough to bite.

On the other side, the marsh moved with its own slow breathing.

The creek murmured like it always had, indifferent to paperwork.

Then the truck's passenger-side window rolled down.

Collins leaned out, cigarette glowing at his mouth. In the truck's dash light, the name patch on his shirt caught the glow.

"Evenin'," he called, voice friendly in the way a trap is friendly. "Little late for a game, ain't it?"

Jack did not speak. His hands curled into fists inside his sleeves. Collins's gaze swept the kids, counting them without appearing to.

"This here's private property," he said.

"You boys got permission?"

Ana stepped forward. "We live here," she said.

"That's permission."

Collins laughed once, low. "That's cute," he replied.

"But it ain't legal."

He flicked ash onto the road. "Tell your old man," he added, looking straight at Jack now, "that Hartwell don't like surprises."

Jack's heart thudded. "We're not surprising anybody," he said.

"You put your flags out in broad daylight."

Collins's smile thinned. "Flags are polite," he said.

"Locks are next."

He let the sentence hang a beat longer than necessary, then raised the window and the truck rolled forward, slow.

When the taillights disappeared, the field felt suddenly too open, too watched. The borrowed lamps hummed. The ribbons snapped.

Eddie's voice came out smaller. "Locks," he whispered.

Jack stared at the stake Ana had notched. "Then we learn to play with locks," he said, and the words surprised him with their steadiness. Ana's hand closed briefly on his wrist—not comforting, exactly.

More like a signal. A promise of partnership.

"Go home," she said.

"And don't tell anyone we were here except Mary."

Jack nodded. He looked down the fence line once more, at the ribbons dancing like warnings.

He did not feel brave. He felt awake. That was worse, and better.

George exhaled once, slow. "Pull it," he said to the man. It wasn't loud. It didn't need to be.

The surveyor looked back, unsure whether George had the authority to give that kind of order. Authority, Jack realized, was mostly a contest of who could stand still the longest.

Collins stepped in front, gentle as a door being closed. "No," he said.

"We have permission."

He reached into his clipboard and produced a folded paper, already creased like it had been practiced. "Right of entry for measurement. Temporary. Legal."

George took the paper but didn't open it. He held it like something that could cut him. "You got a signature," he said.

"From the town," Collins replied.

Mary felt the words settle in her stomach. From the town. As if a town were a person with one hand and one conscience. She wanted to ask whose signature it was. She wanted to ask what it cost. She didn't ask. Not yet.

Asking too soon gave people time to lie.

She opened her ledger instead. The men watched her flip pages like she'd pulled a weapon. She stopped on a blank line and wrote slowly, each letter deliberate enough to count as a decision.

Entry #28—First they draw it. Then they measure it. Then they tell you it was never yours.

She closed the book and looked at Collins. "Who signed?" she asked.

Collins hesitated. The smallest slip—enough to prove he was human. "It's on the document," he said.

"Public record."

"So is my son's name,"

Mary replied.

"Doesn't mean you get to use it."

A car door shut somewhere up the street. Parker Greene walked toward them, coat collar up, eyes already tired. He nodded to George, then to Mary, then to Collins like a man greeting weather.

"You couldn't wait," Parker said to Collins.

Collins's smile returned, relieved. "We are on schedule," he said.

Parker looked at the ribbons snapping along the creek. "Schedule's a funny word," he murmured. Then, louder: "George. Mary. They're within their rights. For now."

"For now," George repeated, tasting the phrase like metal.

Parker's voice dropped. "They're pushing because the council's split. They're trying to make the future feel inevitable." His eyes flicked to Jack. "Don't let it."

Jack swallowed. He wanted to say something brave. Instead he said the only true thing he had. "We were going to play today."

(Sunday Night · Barrow Street)

George came home late, shoulders sagging with the kind of tired that sits in the bones instead of the muscles.

Mary heard his boots on the porch before he came in. She turned the stove down, wiped her hands on a towel, and watched him step into the kitchen as if he were entering a room where words could hit.

"You eat?" she asked.

"Not hungry," he said automatically. Then, seeing her face, he softened. "I grabbed a coffee. That counts for something."

Mary didn't smile. "Coffee doesn't count when you're trying to keep a family standing."

George set his lunch pail down. The metal thunk sounded too loud in the quiet house. The boys were upstairs—Jack in his bed, Eddie likely at his own place, the town's children scattered in their small rooms like seeds in different soil.

George loosened his collar. "Collins was down by the creek again."

Mary's mouth tightened. "Watching."

"Measuring,"

George corrected, as if the word mattered. "He says it's just for access. Just for utility. Like he's doing us a favor."

Mary looked at the sink where dishes waited. Her hands wanted a task. Her mind wanted a plan.

"And Parker?" she asked.

George exhaled. "Parker says don't antagonize. He says if we pull stakes, if we argue, if we make noise, it becomes 'an issue.' "

"It is an issue,"

Mary said. George's eyes flashed. "I know."

The sharpness in his voice startled them both. George rarely raised his voice. When he did, it meant the fear had climbed too high.

Mary lowered her voice on purpose. "Then why are you repeating Parker like he's scripture?"

George's jaw worked. He looked away toward the window, toward the dark yard where the fence could not be seen but could be felt.

"Because I'm tired," he admitted. "Because I worked ten hours and then went down there and watched a man draw a line through our life like it's nothing. Because the mill's laying men off and the school's moving kids like chess pieces and we're still pretending we can hold back everything with boards and nails."

Mary's throat tightened. She wanted to lash back. She wanted to say, You built the fence. You said it would hold.

Instead she stepped closer. "George," she said, and said his name the way you say someone's name when you don't want to lose them.

He rubbed a hand over his face. "I don't want Jack to pay for my pride," he said quietly.

Mary felt something shift. There it was—the truth under the anger. "It's not pride," she replied.

"It's protection."

George's eyes met hers. They were tired eyes. Kind eyes. Eyes that had seen war headlines and bank balances and the inside of a freezer with too little meat.

Mary reached for his hand on the counter. His fingers were cold. "You remember when you asked me to marry you?" she said.

George blinked, caught off guard. "What does that have to do with Hartwell?"

"Answer me."

He swallowed. "I was nineteen," he said.

"I had no money. I had a truck that leaked oil. I told you I couldn't promise you anything but work."

"And I said yes," Mary replied.

George's mouth twitched. "You said yes because you were stubborn."

"I said yes because I believed you,"

Mary corrected. "And because you looked at me like I was home."

George's shoulders slumped a fraction. The fight drained out of him like steam.

Mary took a breath.

"We're doing what we did then," she said.

"Showing up before we're ready and calling it a promise anyway."

George looked at her, raw and tired, as the radio clicked to itself in the other room.

George's throat bobbed. "And if the fence doesn't hold?"

Mary's voice softened. "Then we hold each other," she said.

"And we build again." The kitchen went quiet enough for them to hear the pipes settle in the wall.

George stepped closer. He slid his hand to Mary's waist with the carefulness of a man asking permission even after years. Mary leaned into him, forehead resting briefly against his chest. She could smell cold air and coffee and the faint metal tang of his day.

"I don't want to lose you to this fight," he whispered.

Mary closed her eyes. "Then don't," she whispered back. "Stay."

George's arms tightened, and for a few seconds the world outside the windows—the flags, the papers, the men with pens—did not exist.

Then Mary felt George's heart thudding too fast, too hard. She pulled back and searched his face. "You okay?"

He nodded too quickly. "Just tired."

Mary did not let him escape with that. She reached up and pressed her palm to his cheek, then to his neck, feeling his pulse.

"You're not a machine," she said.

George's smile was small. "I'm not," he admitted. "But some days I have to pretend."

Mary's hand dropped. She turned to the counter where her ledger sat, closed, waiting.

"We don't pretend in this house," she said.

"We name things."

George looked at the ledger, then at Mary. "Name it," he said. Mary picked up her pencil.

Entry #32—Fear makes men loud. Love makes men stay. Tonight, George stayed.

She paused, then added a second line.

Entry #32—If the world wants to move our children like chess pieces, then we become the board they cannot lift.

Mary underlined stay once. George watched her write as if the words could keep him upright.

When she closed the book, he exhaled. "Okay," he said.

"Tomorrow, we plan."

Mary nodded. "Tomorrow," she agreed. "And then the next day.

And then as long as we need."

Outside, the wind pressed against the house like a question. Inside, the Davises answered with quiet hands held together.

George glanced at him, and the hard set of his jaw softened by a fraction. "Then we play," he said.

He walked down the line and picked up the nearest ribbon. For one breath he considered yanking it free. Then he tied it to the fence rail instead, right beside the old carved initials—F.D.—like he was pinning evidence where everyone could see it.

"Measure that," he told Collins.

Collins didn't answer. He didn't have to. The ribbons kept snapping. The creek kept moving. And somewhere in town, a pen had already moved across paper once, and the ink was already dry. (Two Days Later · Parked Buick · Edge of the Marsh)

The Buick sat half on the shoulder, half on dirt. The engine was off. The radio was low. Collins kept one hand on the steering wheel out of habit.

Carver climbed in without knocking, carrying the smell of expensive cologne into the old car like an insult. He tossed a manila envelope onto Collins's lap.

"You look tired," Carver said.

"I have been in mud,"

Collins replied.

"Your shoes would not survive it."

Carver smiled thinly. "Mud washes. Minutes do not."

Collins flipped the envelope open. Inside were photocopied forms—permitting language, hazard signage templates, and a letterhead stamped with county authority.

"We already have this?" he asked.

"We already have the people who can pretend we have this,"

Carver said.

"That is the same thing."

Collins hesitated.

"Ana Morales threatened me today."

Carver's brows lifted, almost amused. "The girl pitcher?"

"She is not a girl when she is mad,"

Collins said.

"She said if we touch the fence again, she will make sure everybody knows."

Carver leaned back and looked through the windshield toward the dark line of trees. "Then we give everybody something else to know," he said.

"A photo. A rumor. A concern. The town loves concern. It makes cruelty feel like care."

Collins swallowed. "You do not have to do it like this."

Carver turned to him, voice dropping. "You think Hartwell is paying you to place stakes?" he asked.

"Hartwell pays you to move a town without ever lifting a shovel."

He tapped the envelope. "Post the sign when Parker says. Call it temporary. Call it for safety. And Collins -"

"What?"

Carver's smile returned. "Do not make threats. Make offers. The only difference is whether the person thinks they are choosing."

Chapter Seven — The Busing Year

©

(Fall 1974 · Saugus / Lynn / Boston on TV)

BY THE FALL OF 1974, the word busing had stopped meaning field trips.

It had become something heavier—shouted on newscasts, painted on signs, spat between neighbors who used to nod at each other in parking lots.

(Next Morning · Barrow Street)

The photograph came in an unmarked envelope.

Mary found it between the grocery circular and a church flyer, tucked into the screen door where the mailman sometimes shoved things when it was damp.

It was a Polaroid—the kind that developed as you watched, the kind that made truth feel immediate.

In the image, Cedarbrook Field lay under borrowed light. The grass looked silver. The infield dirt looked like a bruise. And near the fence line, three boys stood in a small huddle—Jack, Eddie, and Ana, Mary recognized instantly by the angle of her shoulders. They were not doing anything wrong.

They were simply there.

At the bottom of the photo, someone had written in block letters: AFTER HOURS. Mary's fingers went numb.

George came in from outside with the morning paper under his arm. He stopped when he saw her face.

"What is it?"

Mary held up the photograph.

George took the photograph carefully. His eyes scanned the image, then the handwriting.

"They were on the field," he said, voice low. "They were on our field,"

Mary corrected. George's jaw hardened. "Who took it?"

Mary didn't answer because she didn't know. But she could guess the kind of person who would.

She turned the photo over. There was no name. Only a stamped message in faint purple ink:

FOR YOUR RECORDS.

George's nostrils flared.

"Records," he repeated, and the word sounded like a curse. Mary set the photo on the table beside her ledger. She stared at the picture again, seeing not the kids but the story somebody wanted to tell: reckless. Disorderly.

Dangerous. After hours. After rules.

"This is how they do it," she said quietly. "They make being alive look like a violation."

George slammed the paper down. "I'm going down to Parker," he said. Mary caught his wrist. "No," she said.

"Not yet."

He looked at her, eyes hot. "Mary, they're photographing our son like he's a criminal."

Mary's grip tightened. "And if you storm into Parker's office, they'll photograph that too," she said.

"They'll write that down too. They'll call it 'aggressive.' "

George's breath came hard. He wanted to move. He wanted to hit something. He wanted to hammer nails until the world made sense again.

Mary pulled him closer until his anger had nowhere to go but into her shoulder. She held him, firm.

"Listen," she said into his collar. "They want us sloppy. They want us loud. They want us to give them a story they can sell."

George swallowed. "So what do we do?"

Mary stepped back and looked him in the eye. "We make our own record," she said.

She opened her ledger to a fresh page.

Entry #35—They are watching the field with cameras. They are building a case out of childhood.

She paused, pencil hovering as she felt George's gaze on her.

Entry #35—If they want records, we keep better ones.

George exhaled, the fight shifting into focus. "We talk to Krantz," he said.

"We talk to Father Donnelly. We talk to every mother who's ever had a kid chased off a sidewalk for being loud."

Mary nodded. "And we keep the photo," she said.

"Not as shame.

As evidence."

George looked down at the image again. Jack's face was a pale oval under the lights, turned slightly as if he'd heard something behind him. In the photo, it looked like fear.

George's voice softened. "He looks... young."

Mary reached over and touched the corner of the Polaroid. "He is," she said.

"That's why we don't let them turn him into a file."

George looked toward the window, toward the yard, toward the place where the fence stood invisible in morning fog.

"Okay," he said.

"We play smart."

Mary closed the ledger and slid the photograph inside it like a pressed flower. A bitter bloom.

At the top of the stairs, Jack's door creaked. He appeared, hair messy, eyes blinking.

"What's going on?" he asked.

Mary smiled, quick and practiced. "Nothing you need to carry," she said.

Jack's gaze flicked to the ledger. He saw the Polaroid edge tucked inside like a secret.

"I saw a truck last night," he admitted. "On Chestnut. Collins."

George's jaw set. "Did he say anything?"

Jack hesitated. "He said... locks are next."

Mary felt her stomach drop. She kept her face steady. "Then we plan," she said.

Jack looked between them. He was old enough to know when adults were lying. He was young enough to still hope the lie meant safety.

Mary walked to him and smoothed his hair back from his forehead. "You go eat," she said.

"Then you go to school. Let the adults handle the locks."

Jack nodded, but his eyes stayed on the ledger, unsure what it could do and afraid of what it might have to.

When he turned away, Mary looked at George. "Locks," she repeated softly. "Or fear. Or both."

George's hand closed over hers on the table. "Then we make them pay for every inch," he said.

Mary squeezed his fingers. Outside, the morning moved on like it always did. Inside, the Davises began writing a war that would not be fought with guns.

It would be fought with paper, and love, and the stubborn refusal to be erased.

On Chestnut Street, the trees burned orange and red. Leaves dropped in slow spirals onto sidewalks that had carried the same kids to the same schools for years. Now nobody was sure where anyone would end up. New routes were being drawn on maps in offices miles away—bright marker lines sliding across nameless streets, deciding which child sat where without ever asking them.

WBZ carried it every night.

"Federal judge orders Boston schools to integrate by court-mandated busing..."

"Protests erupt in South Boston..."

"Parents line the streets, some cheering, some throwing rocks..."

In Mary Davis's living room, the images flickered across the console TV: yellow buses rocking, kids pressed to the windows, adults' faces warped into something that didn't look like adulthood at all.

George watched from his chair, pipe unlit in his hand.

Jack sat cross-legged on the floor with his back against the couch, eyes level with the chaos.

"Why are they throwing things at the buses?" he asked.

"Because they're scared,"

Mary said from the doorway. "And some people turn scared into mean instead of into questions."

George shifted.

"Some people don't like having lines moved on them," he said.

"They think the way it's been is the way it should always be."

Jack thought about the fence along the creek—how it hadn't always been there and how now it felt like it always had.

On the TV, a commentator traced new school districts with a pen on a map of Boston. Colored lines crossed rivers and stadiums, sliced through neighborhoods whose names they never said out loud.

Grown-ups move lines on paper; kids have to live inside them, Jack thought. He didn't write it down, but it stayed.

The talk at Mrs. Foster's turned from the refinery to buses and judges and words like court-ordered and integration that sat awkwardly on tongues used to back when and the way it's always been. Kay poured coffee and listened.

"I'm just saying," one man at the counter grumbled, "you start moving kids like chess pieces, you're asking for trouble."

"They're not pieces," another man answered.

"They're kids."

"My nephew's getting bused across town," a woman said.

"He's twelve. What's he supposed to do—make a new life because someone with a pen says so?"

"Maybe he'll make a better one," someone else replied.

Mary sat at a side table, ledger closed beside her cup. She watched the lines being drawn in people's faces as much as on the maps.

"It's all lines,"

Kay said quietly, leaning over. "School lines, town lines, zoning lines."

"And every one of them drawn by someone who sleeps just fine afterward,"

Mary said.

"Not everyone,"

Kay answered.

"You don't sleep."

Mary gave a humorless smile. "I dream in ledgers."

Kay nodded toward the window. From here they couldn't see the fence, but they could feel the direction of it—the way you could sense certain landmarks even when they were out of sight.

"World's busy moving lines,"

Kay said.

"Yours is one of the only ones that hasn't budged."

"That's what scares them,"

Mary said.

"And what scares me is they'll find a way around it."

(That Afternoon · Town Hall Steps)

By the time they reached Town Hall, Mary could feel the crowd before she saw it.

Voices spilled out the open doors. Cars lined the curb like an invitation and a warning. The steps were crowded with men in work boots and women in church coats, with teenagers in letterman jackets and children tugging sleeves.

Hartwell had brought friends, Parker had promised.

Mary held the petition bag tight against her side. George walked on her left, Jack on her right, shoulders squared against the world.

Parker stood near the entrance with a clipboard. He looked up as they approached, and for a fraction of a second Mary saw something in his eyes that looked like apology.

"Mary," he said.

"George."

Mary didn't slow. "We're here," she replied.

Parker's gaze dropped to the canvas bag. "Good," he said, but his voice was careful.

They climbed the steps. On the landing, a man Mary didn't recognize stepped into their path. He wore a tie too shiny for the town and cologne too loud. Hartwell's kind.

"Mrs. Davis," he said, smiling with all innocence. "I'm Mr. Carver."

Mary didn't offer her hand. "Then you're in the wrong town," she said.

Carver's smile held. "We prefer to think of it as the right town with... potential," he replied. His eyes flicked to Jack. "And so much youth. It'd be a shame if anyone got hurt playing on... unsafe land."

George's shoulders tensed. "Say what you mean," he said.

Carver's voice stayed light. "I did," he answered.

"We all want what's best for children."

Mary's jaw tightened. She hated when men used children as shields. Parker cleared his throat. "Let them through," he said, sharper than he meant. Carver stepped aside with a theatrical bow.

Inside, the hallway was packed. Mary threaded through bodies, feeling hands brush her sleeve, feeling eyes on the bag.

They reached the meeting room door.

Mary unzipped the bag to check the petition one last time. Her breath left her.

The top pages were gone.

Not misplaced. Not shuffled. Gone. The staple holes remained, ragged as torn skin.

Mary flipped through the stack with shaking fingers. Entire sheets had been ripped out—not the last pages, not random. Specific ones.

The names she'd counted on. The names that had been hardest to get. The names that had promised to stand.

George leaned in. "What?" he whispered. Mary held up the torn edge.

George's face went rigid. "No," he said softly. Jack's eyes widened. "They stole it?"

Mary's mind raced, hunting for when. The porch. The bag at her feet. The moment she'd set it down to tie Jack's collar. A hand. A brush. A smile.

Parker saw their faces and stepped closer. "What happened?"

Mary looked at him. Her voice was calm in the way only fury can make a voice calm.

"Someone took pages," she said.

Parker's eyes flicked to the torn holes. For a second, the mask slipped. "Jesus," he muttered, then caught himself. "I mean... that's serious."

George's hands clenched. "It's sabotage."

Carver appeared at Parker's shoulder. "Problem?" he asked, all innocence.

Mary stared at him.

"You," she said, and it wasn't a question. Carver's smile widened. "Mrs. Davis," he said gently.

"Accusations in public are a poor look."

Mary stepped closer until Carver could smell her anger. "You took pages of my petition," she said.

"You stole names."

Carver lifted his hands. "I would never," he said, and the lie was so smooth it might have been practiced.

Parker's jaw worked. He looked between them, caught between his job and his town and the part of him that still remembered being a boy on that grass.

"We're starting," he said finally. "Get inside."

Mary swallowed the panic that wanted to rise. Panic was what they wanted. Sloppy. Loud. Unhinged.

She forced her hands steady. She closed the bag carefully, trying to hold the torn paper together by will.

Jack whispered, "We're done."

Mary turned to him. Her eyes were fierce. "No," she said.

"We're not done. They didn't take all of it. They took what they feared."

George's voice was low. "What do we do?"

Mary looked at Parker. "You saw me carry it in," she said.

"You will write down that it arrived damaged. You will write down that pages were removed."

Parker hesitated. Carver's gaze sharpened.

Then Parker nodded once. “I’ll note it,” he said.

“For the record.”

Mary held his eyes. “Good,” she replied.

“Because we keep records now.”

She reached into the bag and pulled out the remaining petition pages.

She raised them slightly so the nearest people could see.

“These are the names they couldn’t erase fast enough,” she said, loud enough for the hallway to hear. “And if you signed and your page is missing, you come find me after this meeting. We sign again. We sign louder.”

A murmur ran through the crowd like electricity. Carver’s smile faltered.

Parker looked at Mary, and for a second she saw it: the flicker of respect a man gives a woman who will not be managed.

Jack’s chest rose and fell. He looked scared. He also looked proud. They went into the meeting room with torn paper and full hearts, and Mary understood something new and terrible: Hartwell was not arguing facts. Hartwell was writing a story. So Mary wrote back.

At home, envelopes began arriving from the school district—polite letters, faded maps, and phrases like capacity balancing meant to make disruption sound reasonable.

Mary spread them out on the kitchen table. The new routes spiderwebbed across town, looping past corners Jack knew and cutting through neighborhoods he didn’t.

“Which one am I?” Jack asked, leaning over her shoulder.

She traced the line for their street with her finger. It jumped from one school to another like a skipping record.

“I don’t know yet,” she said. He watched the lines dance. “Why do they keep changing it?” he asked.

“Because they can,”

George said from the doorway. “People with maps and titles can do that.”

Jack’s eyes slid toward the back window, where the fence stood in its usual silent place.

"Fence doesn't move when they redraw maps," he said.

"That's the point,"

George replied.

Later that week, Mary walked Jack down to Cedarbrook. The field was half-mud, half-memory—winter not quite finished, spring not quite brave enough. The fence cut its steady line between grass and marsh.

"Looks the same," Jack said.

"It is the same,"

Mary answered.

"That's the whole argument."

He looked at her. "What do you mean?"

"Some lines you draw with ink," she said.

"Some you draw with wood and sweat.

Only one of those cares who's on the bus."

Jack didn't answer. He was thinking about the kids on the TV, their faces pressed to glass, watching adults decide where they belonged.

That night, after he'd gone to bed, Mary opened her ledger.

She passed over the entries about Hartwell and the refinery and stopped on a fresh line.

Entry #31—Men in offices move lines with pens. Kids pay the bus fare. Our fence is the only line they haven't found a way to move. Yet.

She underlined yet without meaning to, then closed the book.

Outside, the fence stood where it always had, separating the field from the marsh. In a world where so many lines were being redrawn, it felt both comforting and dangerous to have one that refused.

Chapter Eight — The Fence at Night

©

Winter 1974 · Cedarbrook Field, Saugus

THE FIRST TIME JACK realized the fence sounded different at night, he was thirteen and old enough to know better than to be out there alone.

The day had ended in a gray shrug of clouds. By suppertime, the cold had settled in with intent. Mary had told him twice to leave his glove in the mudroom and come to the table. He swore he heard her; he just couldn't make his feet move.

After the dishes were done and WBZ finished its late-edition headlines, the house grew quiet. The kind of quiet Michael had written about from Da Nang—where every noise meant something.

Jack lay in bed, staring at the ceiling. Somewhere down the hall, George coughed once and turned over. Mary's steps moved from kitchen to living room and back again. Then even those faded. He got up, pulled on his boots, and slipped out the back door.

The air hit him like a reprimand—sharp, clean, unforgiving. His breath rose in short bursts and vanished. The houses along Chestnut Street were pockets of yellow, curtains drawn, television light flickering against walls.

Cedarbrook waited in its usual place. The fence cut across the dark like a held breath.

He walked along the worn path, snow crunching underfoot. The creek whispered somewhere beneath thin ice, a sound half water, half memory.

At night, the fence no longer looked like something you leaned on.

It looked like something that divided.

He put his hand on the top rail. The wood was cold enough to sting. Under his fingers, he could feel the faint vibration of the night—wind, distant traffic, the hum of Route 1.

From here, the highway was a low glow in the distance. Neon signs pulsed, promising warm food, cheap rooms, a kind of escape that never lasted past checkout.

Between that glow and this fence lay houses, streetlights, and a town trying to decide what kind of place it wanted to be.

Somewhere beyond the marsh, a car engine idled, then went quiet.

Jack listened.

Headlights appeared on the far side of the field, washing the fence in pale beams for a heartbeat before sliding away. The car didn't move on. It stopped.

He felt the hairs rise on his arms beneath his jacket.

The engine stayed off. The lights stayed dark. The silhouette of the car just sat there—a shape where there hadn't been one before.

"Who's out there?" he called, voice louder than he meant it to be. Silence answered. The creek muttered. A dog barked two streets over.

He stayed still, one hand on the rail. He could feel his own pulse in his fingers.

After a long minute, the car started. Headlights flared, sweeping the boards once more. The vehicle turned and pulled away, tires crunching over gravel.

Jack traced the rail with his hand as the sound faded.

Line between kids heading home and men who never do, he thought.

He didn't know where the thought came from, but once it arrived, it wouldn't leave.

The next night, Parker walked the field with George, hands deep in his coat pockets. "Kids say they saw a car sitting out here,"

Parker said.

"No lights. Just watching."

"Jack,"

George said.

"He was rattled."

"Good,"

Parker replied.

"Means he was paying attention."

They walked the fence line slowly. Boards creaked under the weight of their hands. The night carried all the usual sounds—distant sirens, a train somewhere, the whisper of the river.

"You think it's Hartwell's boys?" George asked.

Parker sniffed. "Hartwell doesn't come out in the cold. He sends men who don't mind getting dirty."

"Winter Hill?"

George said quietly.

Parker took his time answering.

"Word is Hartwell's been promising certain outfits a cut if the refinery goes through," he said.

"Those men like to know the lay of the land ahead of time. Where the lines are. Who might get in the way."

George's jaw clenched. "This fence wasn't built to be a line in someone's ledger."

"It is now,"

Parker said.

"Thing about lines—they look different depending on which side you're on."

They reached the far corner where the fence met the tree line. A beer can lay half-crushed in the snow, fresh tracks leading back to the road.

Parker bent, picked it up, and turned it in his hand.

"Been here since this afternoon?"

George asked. Parker shook his head. "Fresh," he said.

"Cold."

He tossed it into the trash bag he'd brought. "You worried?"

George asked.

"I'd be dumber than I look if I wasn't,"

Parker said.

"But we're not alone. Remember that."

That night, Mary sat at the kitchen table with the ledger open. The lamp cast a small circle of light over the pages, leaving the rest of the room in a kind of quiet dusk.

"What are you writing?"

George asked, coming in from checking the locks. "Same thing I always write," she said.

"Proof that we were here. Proof that we didn't just let things happen to us."

He watched as she put the pen to the page.

Entry #34—Fence will not fall quietly. Neither will we.

She underlined will not once.

"Think that's a little dramatic?"

George asked, half teasing. Mary looked up at him. "I don't," she said.

"Not anymore."

Later, when the house had gone quiet again, Jack lay in bed listening to the wind move around the eaves. Every creak sounded like a footstep. Every car passing on the road sounded like one that might stop.

He pictured the fence cutting through the dark, holding the town's side of the world against whatever lived in the marsh and the roads beyond.

Out there, he thought, men he'd never met were measuring the field in dollars and leverage. In here, his mother was measuring it in names and promises.

He decided he trusted her ledger more.

Chapter Nine — The Petition

©

(February 1974 · Saugus Town Hall / Mrs. Foster's / Route 1 Corridor)

THE FIRST TIME MARY signed a petition, she was young enough to confuse paper with virtue. This time she knew better. Paper could save a place, and paper could dress a lie in a clean collar. The difference was who got there first.

Hartwell's revised zoning petition—73-A—meant the refinery was back, only better scrubbed. The language was softer. The maps were prettier. The harm was the same.

Between now and the hearing, the town would decide what kind of line it wanted on its own map.

Mary intended to give it names before Hartwell gave it acreage. She didn't start at Town Hall. She started on her street.

"Who first?" Jack asked, the clipboard tucked under one arm like he had been born carrying errands that mattered.

"The people who feed other people before they tell them what to think,"

Mary said.

"Those are the ones a town trusts."

Mrs. Romano answered the door with flour on her hands and sauce on her apron. Mary kept the explanation to the three words that did the work: Hartwell. Refinery. Zoning.

Mrs. Romano took the clipboard before Mary had fully finished. "My boys learned to run on that field," she said, signing hard enough to dent the page. "If Hartwell wants to pave something, let him start with his own driveway."

Mr. O'Rourke listened with his arms folded, newspaper tucked under one elbow. "People say refinery means jobs," he said.

"People say a lot when someone buys them coffee,"

Mary answered.

"They're not putting this thing in Melrose. They're putting it where they think tired people will swallow it."

He held out his hand for the pen. "My lungs did their time," he said.

"I'm not asking my grandkids to do the next shift."

Not every door opened into agreement.

Mrs. Kane stood in her doorway with one hand braced against the frame, already apologizing with her eyes before she spoke. Her brother had been out of work six months. Men were whispering that Hartwell's project meant hires.

"They're not saying whose kids stand downwind," Mary said.

Mrs. Kane's mouth tightened. "Some of us can't afford to be on the wrong side of the wrong men," she answered. She did not sign.

Mary marked the refusal with a small pencil note, not as punishment. As record.

At Mrs. Foster's, Kay signed before Mary had the petition fully unrolled.

"I need names people recognize," Mary said.

"Then start with people who can still smell smoke from here,"

Kay replied, sliding the clipboard to one of the regulars by the window. "You complain about your lungs every morning. Here's your chance to do something besides cough."

That got a laugh, which helped. Laughter loosened hands.

A man named Tony hesitated over the line. "Refinery means work," he said.

"Got a cousin says they pay good."

"Pay good now,"

Kay said.

"Then charge your kid for the breathing later."

Tony looked at Mary. "How many names you got?"

"Enough to make them notice," she said.

"Not enough to make them nervous yet."

He signed. "Then make them nervous."

By week's end the clipboard held a cross-section of the town—names from triple-deckers and split-levels, from the marsh side and the hill side, from people who had lived there forever and people still learning how to pronounce Saugus without feeling like outsiders.

The pattern was plain. The closer a house sat to the creek, the smell, the truck route, the proposed site, the easier the pen moved.

Jack flipped through the pages at the kitchen table. "Is it enough?" he asked.

Mary stacked the sheets, squared the corners, and felt the weight of every yes and every refusal. "It's enough to make them count people before they count dollars," she said.

He looked at the names again. "And if they still don't?"

Mary slipped the packet into her bag. "Then we make them say no out loud where the whole town can hear it."

She took a last look out the window at the boards along the creek, then turned out the kitchen light.

"We ready?" George asked.

"As we're ever going to be," she said.

Jack straightened his collar. Parker waited on the porch, hands in his coat pockets, eyes on the road.

"Town Hall's going to be full," he said.

"Hartwell's bringing friends."

"So are we,"

Mary replied.

She patted the bag at her side, feeling the weight of every name inside.

(The Next Morning · Town Clerk's Office)

Town Hall smelled like paper that had been handled too many times— ink, dust, and other people's decisions. Mary stood at Parker's counter with her coat still on, as if refusing to settle meant refusing to accept what she had come for.

Parker did not look up right away. He was rewriting something by hand even though the typewriter sat two feet away. The old habit of making the record look personal.

"You said you would note it,"

Mary said.

"I did,"

Parker replied.

Mary slid yesterday's copy of the minutes toward him. The line she had been waiting for was not there. Where she expected: Petition arrived damaged, pages removed. Where she expected: suspected tampering.

Instead, the sentence read: Petition submitted incomplete.

Mary felt heat climb her neck. "Incomplete," she said.

"That is your word?"

Parker finally met her eyes. Under the fluorescent light he looked older than he had yesterday. Tired in a way that was not just work.

"Carver was in my office after you left," he said quietly. Mary's laugh was sharp. "Of course he was."

"He reminded me,"

Parker continued, "that the town has liability exposure. He reminded me that if I put certain language in the minutes, it becomes evidence."

"It already is evidence,"

Mary snapped. "It happened."

Parker's jaw tightened. "He reminded me," he said, voice lowering further, "that my name is on things I did when I was younger. Things I do not want dragged out on the courthouse steps."

Mary stared at him. The apology she had seen in his eyes yesterday felt like a lie now, or worse—a truth that had been bought.

"So you changed the record," she said.

Parker's shoulders lifted a fraction, the smallest surrender. "I softened it."

"You did not soften it,"

Mary said.

"You turned it."

Parker opened his mouth, then closed it again. The silence between them was a fence post set deeper than either had expected.

"You want to know what your minutes just did?"

Mary said.

"They gave Hartwell permission to say we cannot even keep our own papers straight."

Parker looked down. "Mary -"

"Keep your minutes," she said.

"I will keep my ledger."

At the door she paused. "And when you decide which side of your own town you live on," she added, "do not send a note. Come stand where people can see you."

Chapter Ten — Winter Hill Whispers

©

(March 1974 · North Shore, Massachusetts)

AFTER THE HEARING, THE town did something rare: it exhaled.

The council chambers had been packed, the air thick with sweat, cheap cologne, and anger.

(Two Days Later · Mary's Kitchen)

The call came before dawn, when the house still belonged to quiet and the world outside had not yet remembered its cruelty.

Mary answered on the second ring, expecting Mrs. Foster or the mill—expecting something local, something she could hold.

Instead, a man's voice said, "Mrs. Davis?"

Mary sat up straighter. "Yes."

"This is Halpern. From Environmental."

Mary's throat tightened. George was still asleep beside her, one arm flung across the pillow like a boy. Mary did not wake him yet. She listened.

"We ran the samples," Halpern said. His voice sounded careful, like he was reading from a script he didn't fully agree with.

"And?" Mary asked.

There was a pause. The line crackled faintly. "The numbers aren't... clean," he said.

Mary's fingers curled around the receiver. "What does that mean?"

"It means there are contaminants above what we like to see,"

Halpern replied.

"Not catastrophic.

But enough that if someone wanted to make an argument about... safety... they could."

Mary closed her eyes. In her mind, she saw Carver's smile. "Is it from the creek?" she asked.

"From the field?"

Halpern hesitated. "The creek runs past Route 1," he said slowly. "It runs past the old industrial lots. Runoff doesn't ask who owns what."

Mary's jaw tightened. "So you don't know."

"We know the sample. We don't know the story," Halpern said, and there was a softness there now, a hint of apology.

Mary stared at the dark kitchen. "Who else has the results?" she asked. Halpern's silence was answer enough.

Mary's voice sharpened. "Halpern."

He exhaled. "The report goes to the council," he admitted. "And Parker requested a copy."

Mary's stomach dropped. Parker had requested it. Parker had a folder. Parker had access. Parker had a way of turning numbers into weapons.

Mary squeezed her eyes shut until she saw white.

"Mrs. Davis," Halpern said, and now he sounded like a man trying to step back from the edge of something he'd been pushed toward. "I'm calling because... because I grew up on a field like yours. And because I don't want you blindsided."

Mary's voice softened by a fraction. "What are you telling me?"

"I'm telling you," he said, "that they can make this sound worse than it is. They can use words like hazard and liability. They can scare mothers who just want their kids home safe."

Mary opened her eyes and looked at the ledger on the table. Even in the dark, it waited.

"What would you do?" she asked.

Halpern paused. "I'd get your own test," he said.

"Independent.

Someone not paid by Hartwell or afraid of the council." Mary nodded, though he could not see. "Okay."

"And," Halpern added, voice dropping, "I'd watch your mailbox.

People get brave when they think science is on their side." Mary's throat tightened. "Thank you," she said, and meant it.

When she hung up, she sat still for a moment, listening to George's breathing in the bedroom.

The world outside was silent.

Then, faintly, she heard it: the click of a handset in another room.

Mary's blood went cold.

Someone—Jack? No. Jack slept like a rock. Eddie wasn't here. No one else should be on the line.

Mary rose without turning on the light. She moved down the hall, steps soft.

The phone in the den sat on the side table. The receiver was not fully down. It hovered, crooked.

Mary stared at it, heart pounding.

She pressed it down gently until it clicked.

Then she stood there in the dark, understanding the new shape of their fight. They were not just being watched.

They were being listened to.

Mary returned to the kitchen and opened her ledger with shaking hands.

Entry #39—They will use numbers as weapons. They will use fear as proof.

They will listen at our doors.

She paused, pencil hovering, then wrote the next line harder.

Entry #39—We will not be afraid in silence.

Mary underlined not be afraid twice.

In the bedroom, George shifted in his sleep. Mary looked toward him, and her love for him rose sharp and fierce—not gentle tonight, but protective, like a fence.

She walked back and touched his shoulder. "George," she whispered. He blinked awake, confused. "What?"

Mary held his gaze in the dim light. "They have the water report," she said.

"And someone just listened on our phone."

George sat up fully. The tiredness fell away.

Neither of them moved. The refrigerator motor kicked on, loud as a warning, and the house stopped feeling like shelter.

Then George reached for Mary's hand, and his grip was steady. "Okay," he said quietly. "Then we get louder than their listening."

Mary nodded.

Outside, dawn pressed at the window. Inside, the Davises made a decision that no longer needed saying aloud.

Hartwell could bring suits, experts, and diagrams.

Mary would bring petitions. George would bring the part of himself that no longer cared about being reasonable first.

Voices shook. Then steadied. In the end, the vote went their way.

Article 73-A: Denied.

For a few weeks, it felt like victory might be permanent.

Survey flags disappeared. Providence trucks stopped idling at corners. The air around the creek smelled like salt and mud again instead of anxiety.

"Maybe they're finally getting the message," George said one night, resting his hand on the top rail of the fence.

Parker didn't smile.

"Men like Hartwell don't hear 'no,' " he said.

"They hear 'not yet.' "

Mary heard him. She didn't argue.

The first phone call came on a Tuesday just after nine.

Mary had just closed the ledger and turned off the kitchen light when the phone rang in the living room. The sound cut through the house like a blade.

George answered.

"Davis residence."

Silence at first. Then a male voice, smooth as a radio announcer, slipped through the line.

"You fought hard at that hearing, Mr. Davis," it said.

"Impressive."

George's grip tightened on the receiver.

"Who is this?" he asked.

"A neighbor," the voice said.

"Someone who appreciates effort. We wanted to let you know there are still opportunities. Council votes can change. Deals can be...re-framed."

"We're not interested,"

George said.

"You might be if you saw the numbers on the table," the man replied.

"Hartwell's done well for himself. He knows how to share."

"We already share,"

George said.

"With our kids." There was a soft chuckle.

"Think about it," the caller said.

"You people build fences. We build futures. Lot more money in futures."

The line went dead.

George stood there for a long moment, receiver still in his hand. "Who was it?" Mary asked from the doorway.

"Wrong number," he said.

She didn't believe him. She also didn't press. Not yet.

The second call came two days later in the middle of dinner.

Jack was halfway through a plate of pasta when the phone shrilled.

Mary went to answer this time, wiping her hands on a dish towel. "Hello?"

"Mrs. Davis," the same smooth voice said.

"Glad I caught you."

"You didn't," she said.

"You interrupted."

The man laughed like they were sharing a joke.

"Wanted you to know there are people in Somerville who can help make your problems go away," he said.

"Disputes. Zoning issues. That sort of thing."

"We don't have a problem,"

Mary said.

"We have a fence."

"Exactly," he replied.

"The kind of thing that can be...addressed. A little persuasion. Some pressure.

Maybe a fire. Nobody wants that." Mary's free hand clenched. "You threatening my home?" she asked.

"Just talking about possibilities," he said.

"Be a shame if something happened to that nice field. Kids get upset when their toys break."

"Kids aren't toys," she snapped. There was a pause. When he spoke again, his tone had cooled.

"Your husband said he wasn't interested in talking numbers," the man said.

"Figured you might be more practical."

"You figured wrong,"

Mary said.

"And if you ever call here again, I'll make sure your name's written in six different ledgers before sunrise."

She hung up before he could answer.

Her hand shook when she put the phone back on the hook. She stared at it for a long beat, then turned.

Jack and George were watching from the doorway. "Who was it?" Jack asked.

"Wrong kind of neighbor,"

Mary said.

"The kind who doesn't live here and never will."

They met Parker at Mrs. Foster's the next morning.

"Winter Hill," he said after hearing their description. "Phone calls like that? That's how they introduce themselves."

"You're sure?"

George asked. Parker stirred his coffee slowly.

"Somerville accent. Too interested in 'opportunities.' Talking like he's doing you a favor. That's their style."

Kay leaned in. "Hartwell's dragged in muscle," she said.

"Saw some new faces at Town Hall that night. Didn't look like they were there for zoning."

Parker nodded.

"Hartwell's a handshake with a knife," he said.

"These boys are the ones who swing it."

Jack swallowed.

"What do they want?" he asked.

Parker looked at him. "Same thing Hartwell wants. The marsh. The creek. The field. They want to carve it up and turn it into money."

"Then why the calls?"

Mary asked.

"Why not just show up and start breaking things?"

"Fear's cheaper than concrete,"

Parker said.

"Phone calls cost a dime. Fires leave evidence."

He looked at George.

"We should go see them," he said quietly. "See who?"

Jack asked.

"The men behind the voice,"

Parker answered.

"Better to know what kind of storm you're facing before it hits."

Mary's stomach turned.

"You can't be serious," she said.

"I'm not leaving some faceless voice leaning over your phone," he replied.

"If they're going to lean on us, I want to see what they lean with."

"Parker—" she began.

He cut her off gently. "I'm not going alone. But I'm not letting them think we scare that easy."

George met his eyes. There was a long moment where everything unsaid sat between them. "When?"

George asked.

"Tomorrow," Parker said. Somerville looked different up close.

The next afternoon, they drove in Parker's truck—a body-red Chevy that had seen better winters. The streets narrowed. Triple-deckers leaned into each other over cracked sidewalks. Bars with dark windows sat between corner stores and laundromats. Kids played stickball in alleys, moving only when a car nosed its way through.

Parker parked in front of a nondescript brick building with a neon beer sign in the window.

"This is stupid," George said under his breath.

"Absolutely,"

Parker replied.

"But not as stupid as pretending this isn't happening."

Inside, the bar smelled like old beer and older decisions. A television muttered in one corner. A few men at the rail turned to look, eyes doing the quick math of strangers.

A man in a leather jacket with careful hair and careful hands approached.

"You're lost," he said.

"We're from Saugus,"

Parker replied.

"Got a call from a friend of yours. About a fence."

The man studied them, slow and deliberate.

"Maybe you did," he said finally. "And maybe you didn't. Either way, you shouldn't be here."

"We don't like anonymous calls,"

George said.

"You got something to say, you say it with a face." A flicker of respect—or amusement—passed through the man's eyes.

"You the ones fighting Hartwell?" he asked.

"We're the ones building a fence,"

Parker said. The man smiled without warmth.

"Hartwell's got plans," he said.

"Plans that involve your creek. He asked us to make sure nothing gets in the way."

"Nothing?"

George asked.

"Nothing that can't be moved," the man answered. Parker stepped closer, keeping his voice level.

"Here's your problem," he said.

"You boys see a fence and think 'obstacle.' We see a fence and think 'promise.' "

The man's smile thinned. "You think a promise means something to us?"

"I think it means something to everyone watching,"

Parker said.

"You start pushing kids around a town like ours, people notice. And folks like you don't like attention that isn't paid in cash."

A silence settled over the bar. Glass clinked somewhere in the back.

The man shrugged. "You're making this harder than it has to be," he said.

"Hard's all we've got," Parker replied. He turned to go. George followed.

At the door, the man called after them.

"Preacher came through here last week," he said.

"Said something about Judas and silver. Told him silver spends the same either way."

Parker glanced back.

"Preacher was right about one thing," he said.

"You don't get to keep it."

They stepped out into the weak afternoon light.

That Sunday, the sermon at St. Margaret's landed harder than most.

"Judas wasn't in the story to be a villain," the priest said.

"He was there to remind us how easy it is to trade what's right for what's easy. Thirty pieces of silver then. Tax breaks, contracts, and quiet deals now."

Mary sat straighter in the pew.

Around her, some shifted, uncomfortable. Some stared at the floor.

Some nodded.

Jack listened, thinking of the bar in Somerville he hadn't been allowed to see and the fence he saw every day.

After Mass, people gathered in the parking lot, conversations low but charged.

"You think Father was talking about Hartwell?" someone asked.

"If he wasn't, he missed a good chance," someone else replied. Mary didn't answer. She didn't need to. The line was drawn.

The story broke on WBZ a week later.

"Investigative team has obtained records suggesting links between Providence Development Partners and known Winter Hill associates..."

Footage of the bar in Somerville. Names half-bleeped. Phrases like organized crime, front company, municipal corruption.

In the Davis living room, the TV light painted their faces blue and white.

"Guess the preacher's sermon traveled," George said. Parker called five minutes later.

"Fear's a quiet weapon," he said.

"But it hates bright lights."

Mary opened the ledger with hands that still trembled a little.

She flipped past entries about Hartwell's visit, the hearing, the latenight calls. She found a clean line.

Entry #45—Fear drowns in company. She wrote it slowly, the ink dark and sure.

Then she added:

Entry #46—Men who trade a town for silver never get to spend it the way they think.

She closed the book and looked at Jack.

"This isn't over," she said.

"But they're not whispering anymore. Now the whole town can hear." Down by the creek, the fence stood its ground. The boards didn't know about Winter Hill or

Hartwell or silver or votes. They knew only how to hold a line between one world and another. That was enough—for now.

(Sunday Morning · Mrs. Foster's Booth · Route 1)

The newspaper lay on the table like a dare. Somebody had folded it to the local page and left it there for Mary to find, the way people leave a knife on a cutting board—not accidental, not kind.

The headline was smaller than the war headlines and bigger than it had any right to be: UNSAFE PLAY: TOWN FACES LIABILITY OVER UNPERMITTED FIELD.

A photo sat beneath it—a blur of kids and borrowed light. The words AFTER HOURS were visible even in black and white.

George's coffee stopped halfway to his mouth. Jack read the first paragraph and felt his stomach drop.

"Unnamed town official," Mary said aloud, voice flat. She did not need to be told whose name was hiding behind those words.

Kay Delios came over with the syrup and saw Mary's expression. "They printed it," she said, not a question.

"They framed it," Mary answered. She scanned the quote again. The phrasing was careful, designed to sound like concern. Designed to make defense sound like recklessness.

George set the mug down. His hands were steady. His eyes were not. "They want parents afraid," he said.

"They want me to look like I am gambling with children,"

Mary replied. She folded the paper precisely, as if neatness could undo damage. Then she looked up. "Fine."

Jack blinked. "Fine?"

"If they want a story,"

Mary said, "we give them one they cannot edit."

She slid out of the booth. "We invite the reporter to Cedarbrook. Today. Not for a speech. For a walk. For names. For splinters. For the truth under their shoes."

George rose with her before Jack did. He did not reach for her hand. He just fell into step beside her, which in that house meant the same thing.

Chapter Eleven — The Water Sample

©

(Winter 1975 · The Creek)

THE COLD THAT WINTER didn't arrive all at once. It crept in the way bad news does—first a thin rim of ice on the creek, then a deeper hush in the morning air, then the kind of wind that made a man tuck his chin and think about shelter.

Jack saw the stranger because he was up early. The field trained you to notice small movements: a runner leaning, a bird dipping, a hand twitching before a throw.

The man wore waders and a knit cap pulled low. He moved along the creek with a practiced caution, stepping where the mud looked firm and stopping where it looked like it might give. He carried a small metal case and a glass jar that caught the pale light like a warning.

Jack stayed behind the fence at first, fingers hooked through the rail. The work-lights were off. The field was empty. It was the hour when the place felt like it belonged to the dead as much as the living.

The man knelt, broke the ice with the end of a rod, and dipped the jar into the water. He held it up and squinted through it like he could read the future in what it caught.

Mary saw him from the kitchen window and was outside before she finished tying her sweater. George followed, slower, like the cold stiffened more than his joints.

"Morning," Mary called, not friendly, not cruel. Just present.

The man startled. He hadn't expected witnesses. "Ma'am," he said. "I'm with an environmental consulting firm. Routine sampling."

"For who?" Mary asked.

His eyes flicked toward George, then back. "For the town," he said, and Jack heard the same phrase Collins had used. As if the town were a single mouth and not a hundred.

George stepped closer, boots crunching frozen grass. "You got paperwork?"

The man opened his case and produced a badge clipped to a laminated card. His name was printed in black: R. Halpern. Below it, smaller: Certified Water Quality Technician.

"And you got permission," George said, not a question.

Halpern nodded once. "Public land. Public interest."

He looked toward the fence like he was trying to be respectful. "It's precautionary.

Rumors."

"Rumors," Mary repeated.

Halpern hesitated. "People are saying the creek isn't what it used to be. That something's coming off Route 1. That the proposed development —"

"Hartwell," Jack said before he could stop himself.

Halpern glanced at him, surprised to find the kid had names. "Potential industrial runoff," he said carefully. "If there's nothing, there's nothing. But if there is, the town needs to know."

Mary felt her throat tighten. The phrase 'the town needs to know' sounded noble until you remembered who got to speak for the town.

"And if there is?" she asked.

Halpern looked down at the jar, now cloudy with disturbed sediment. "Then there'll be recommendations," he said.

"Restrictions. Warnings."

"On us,"

George said.

"On the field."

"On the water," Halpern corrected, but it wasn't a comfort. "I'm not your enemy, Mr. Davis. I'm just doing my job."

George laughed once, without humor. "So am I," he said. He pointed down the fence line where the bright survey ribbons still hung like injuries. "That's my job."

Mary stepped closer to Halpern, lowering her voice so it didn't turn into a performance. "Who ordered this?" she asked.

"The council?"

Halpern's jaw flexed. "A committee," he said.

"I don't know the politics."

Mary almost believed him. Almost. Politics, she thought, is what people call it when they don't want to say greed.

Jack watched the jar in Halpern's hand and imagined it poured out on a desk somewhere, strangers leaning in to decide what was safe. He hated that the field could be judged by a jar.

Mary did something rarer: she reached for George's hand.

It was cold. It was calloused. It shook once before it steadied under her fingers.

"Finish," she told Halpern. "Do your sampling. Then tell us what you find."

Halpern nodded, relieved. "I will," he said. Then, softer: "For what it's worth—I grew up playing on a field like this."

George's eyes narrowed. "Then you know what you're holding," he said.

Halpern looked at the jar again, and for a moment the practiced officialness fell away. "Yeah," he admitted. "I do."

He walked down the creek bank to take another sample. Mary and George stood at the fence without speaking. Jack stayed with them, feeling older and smaller at the same time.

Across the street, a porch curtain twitched. Somebody was watching. Mary knew that kind of watching. It wasn't curiosity. It was accounting.

(That Afternoon · Hartwell Conference Room)

A glass pitcher of water sat untouched in the center of the table, a joke no one laughed at.

Carver laid the lab report down like scripture. Across from him, a young consultant in a stiff suit kept glancing at the numbers, afraid they might accuse him.

Collins arrived late, mud still on his boots, and took the seat nearest the door. "So,"

Carver said, tapping the report. "What are we calling this?"

"The results are mixed," the consultant said.

"Within range in some samples. Slightly elevated in others."

"Ambiguous is the enemy of urgency,"

Carver replied.

"Parents do not mobilize for ambiguous."

"We cannot fabricate," the consultant began.

"We do not fabricate,"

Carver said smoothly. "We interpret."

He circled a line with his pen. "This number. This phrase. 'Above recommended.' That becomes the headline. We do not say the marsh does it. We say, 'until further notice.' The town loves a notice."

Collins shifted. "Davis is going to fight it."

"Of course she is,"

Carver replied.

"That is the beauty. A woman with a ledger arguing with a lab report? We win before she opens her mouth."

"There is one thing," the consultant said quietly, lowering his voice. "Old drums. We picked up traces near the creek that suggest historical dumping."

Carver's smile thinned. "Whose dumping?"

"Unknown," the consultant said.

"Could predate Hartwell. Could predate everyone."

For the first time, Carver looked genuinely interested. "Then we keep that quiet," he said.

"Because if the past gets loud, it starts naming people."

He glanced at Collins. "And people do not like being named." Collins stared at the water pitcher. He thought of boys in the dark.

He thought of the fence that did not move. He thought of how easy it was to move a town with a sentence.

"Draft the advisory,"
Carver said.
"Make it sound like care. Care sells better than fear."

Chapter Twelve — The Winter Letters

©

(1976–1977 · SAUGUS, MASSACHUSETTS) (1976–1977 · Saugus, Massachusetts) WBZ 1030, 5:58 a. m.:

"Cold start across the North Shore. Single digits inland, teens along the coast. Watch for black ice on untreated surfaces, and check on elderly neighbors as we head into the holiday stretch..."

Mary listened with one ear while the other half of her attention went to the kettle, the radiators, and the sound of the house waking up around her. Pipes ticked. The furnace coughed. The wind found every seam in the old clapboards.

On the telephone pole at the end of Chestnut Street, the notice about Article 17 had curled at the edges. The bold black type had faded to a tired gray:

ARTICLE 17—REZONING PETITION (INDUSTRIAL / RECREATIONAL) STATUS: CONTINUED

Continued. Reviewed. Tabled. Grown-ups had a lot of words for not deciding.

Hartwell's campaign caps had gone dull, too. The white thread on the brims had frayed. A few lay abandoned in gutters, soaked in snowmelt and exhaust. The first rush of refinery pamphlets had thinned to a trickle.

But the issue hadn't gone away. It had just gone indoors, into offices where the minutes were typed up and the real conversations weren't.

That was what winter did to trouble in New England—it pushed it behind doors and made it look smaller than it was.

Mary answered by writing.

She wrote to the town clerk, asking when Article 17 would come back to the floor.

She wrote to the state environmental office, asking how much runoff a refinery would send into a marsh like Cedarbrook.

She wrote to WBZ's "Call for Action" segment, enclosing copies of petitions and hearing notes.

She wrote to the editor of the local paper, reminding them that Cedarbrook wasn't an "undeveloped parcel" but a field with names and stories.

Some letters came back stamped RECEIVED. Some came back with careful, polite replies that said very little. Some vanished into whatever drawers took in the voices of people who didn't sign their names with titles.

Still, she kept writing.

Jack watched them accumulate—a stack of carbon copies in a folder by the ledger. Different paper. Same handwriting.

"You think they read all of them?" he asked one night, leaning on the table while she folded a new envelope.

"I think they read enough to know we're not going away," she said. "That's a start."

"What if nothing changes?" he asked.

"Then they have to ignore us on purpose," she replied. "That's different than forgetting we exist."

He wasn't sure it was different enough, but he let it stand.

Winter sat down hard that year and didn't seem inclined to get back up.

By January, the snow at the edge of the road had turned into gray walls. Salt dusted everything that moved. The creek wore a skin of ice that looked solid until the wind shifted and you could hear it moan underneath.

George coughed more in the mornings. He blamed dust, age, the factory. Mary blamed everything and nothing and kept the medicine where she could find it in the dark.

Jack kept going to the field.

On days when the air hurt to breathe, he still walked the line of the fence, boots crunching along the frozen path kids had worn into the grass before the first snow. The boards were streaked with ice where meltwater had run and frozen again. But they stayed straight. He would stop at the spot where the ground dipped toward the creek and stare out at the marsh, trying to picture what it would look like with smokestacks and pipes instead of reeds and cattails.

He couldn't make the picture stick. The field got in the way.

One Saturday, he stood in the kitchen doorway of the Davis house and watched George and Mary without announcing himself.

George sat at the table, rubbing a small circle at the base of his thumb like the ache there had become a habit. Mary bent over the ledger, glasses perched low on her nose, lips moving as she double-checked a column of dates.

They'd both gotten older in the same years the fence had.

He thought of the way the boards had weathered—going from raw, bright cedar to gray that matched the winter sky. First they'd looked new. Now they looked inevitable.

Later that week, he stood with Parker at the backstop, breath hanging in the air between them.

"The fence is starting to look like it grew there," Jack said. Parker squinted along the line.

"Means we did it right," he said.

"People forget there was ever a time without it."

"It's more than boards,"

Jack said quietly.

Parker looked over.

"Say that again," he said.

Jack shrugged, embarrassed. "It's... a line. Between what we say we are and what we'll put up with."

Parker smiled, not unkindly.

"You sound like Mary Davis with a glove on," he said.

"That's a compliment."

Letters came in the other direction, too. Not from offices. From people.

From a teacher who'd read about the fight in the paper and wanted to know if her civics class could come see the field.

From a man in Peabody whose lungs were failing after years at a plant just like the one Hartwell wanted.

From a former Saugus kid now living three states away who'd heard Cedarbrook mentioned on WBZ and wanted to send a check "for whatever you need to keep that fence standing."

Mary kept those letters in a separate stack, tucked between pages of the ledger—a different kind of record.

On a particularly brutal January night in 1977, when the wind sounded like it was trying to scrub the paint off the house and the phone had been silent for weeks, she spread both stacks out on the table: the official replies with their seals and signatures. And the personal ones with their crooked handwriting and coffee stains.

Jack wandered in, rubbing sleep from his eyes.

"More news from Boston?" he asked.

"From everywhere," she said.

He picked up one envelope at random and read the first lines, lips moving silently over the words.

"Do you ever get tired of writing?" he asked.

"Every day," she said.

"Then why keep doing it?"

She looked past him, out the window toward the dark shape of the fence.

"Because ink lasts longer than weather," she said.

"And because someday someone's going to open a file and see our names and realize we didn't let this happen quietly."

She turned to a clean line in the ledger.

Entry #52—Winter is a long pause where men in offices hope we give up.

We answer with letters and boards. Both leave marks.

She let the ink dry and closed the book.

Outside, snow gathered along the fence, soft and relentless. The boards took the weight in silence. Inside, the letters waited. Not finished. Not forgotten.

Across town, in a smaller house that had its own view of the creek if you leaned the right way out the back door, Jack lay in bed and listened to the wind.

He thought about the space between what his parents could see on the news and what they insisted on believing anyway—that good people, working together, could still keep one small thing honest.

It felt about the same size as the distance between their back door and the first post along the creek. Not big. Not small.

Just enough for a line.

Part Three — The Line That Holds

©

(1975–1979)

Chapter Thirteen — The Flood and the Gun

©

(Late Spring 1974 · Saugus, Massachusetts)

BY LATE WINTER, THE snow started melting in strange places first.

It didn't disappear evenly, like a blanket pulled back in one clean motion. It thinned along the fence line, sank into ruts where kids' boots had pounded paths in November, opened puddles in low spots where the creek's breath was warmest. Thin skins of water formed over ice, turning the fence into a wavering double—one line of boards above, one ghost line below.

Mary stood at the kitchen window and watched Jack trace the edges of the puddles with the toe of his boot on his way to school. His book bag bounced against his hip; his head was down, eyes on the reflected fence instead of the road.

"Careful," she murmured, though he was already gone.

On the table behind Mary, the ledger lay open to a fresh page. She had written only the date. The rest, she suspected, would arrive wet.

By late spring the rain no longer came in weather. It came in decisions. The air thickened. The light flattened. The whole house seemed to wait with its shoulders up.

When the storm finally broke, the roof did not sound rained on. It sounded tested.

From the kitchen window Mary watched the creek stop pretending to be modest. Water climbed the bank, took branches with it, then trash, then whole pieces of somebody else's yard. The posts nearest the marsh stood in it like stubborn teeth.

"The creek's too high," she said.

George came to the window and knew from one look that this was not one of the old familiar rises. He reached for his coat. Mary was already reaching for the phone.

By the time George reached the field, rain was coming sideways.

Parker's truck nosed in behind him as far as the mud would allow.

They worked with what men always worked with when the bigger thing had already chosen its size: rope, sandbags, hammers, bad footing, and the refusal to leave a line unattended.

"This isn't a storm anymore,"

Parker said, slinging rope around a post. "It's an inventory."

"Then let it count us standing here," George answered.

Back at the house, Jack pressed his forehead to the glass and watched lightning make two fences out of one—the real rails, and the shaking reflection below them.

The next morning the flood peaked. Drains gave up. The infield disappeared. Only the top rails and backstop still drew the idea of a field above the water.

Nobody stopped Jack then. He pulled on boots, grabbed a shovel, and went.

He worked the inside of the line with George and Parker, cutting channels where water might run off once the creek finally tired of conquest. Mud sucked at every step. Every shovel full weighed more than it looked.

At the low corner by the marsh, Jack's boot struck something metal.

Parker heard it in his voice and came over. Together they scraped mud back with the care people use when they are no longer sure whether they are digging up junk or consequence.

Metal flashed under the water. Then the shape resolved all at once: grip, barrel, trigger guard. A gun.

Parker's face changed first. "Step back," he said.

He worked it loose with both hands and wrapped it in an old towel from the truck. The creek had kept it a long time. It did not look eager to let it go.

Uniforms came first. Then plainclothes. By afternoon the low corner of Cedarbrook looked like a crime scene people had stumbled into ten years late.

That night the district attorney said the words Red Coach Grill on television and the room went still around them.

The weapon, he explained, matched the ballistic record from the 1969 robbery. No new charges would follow. Too much time, too many other convictions, too much law between the act and the naming of it. But the record could now be completed.

Mary sat with her hands locked together in her lap. George leaned forward as if he could force the years to close up by staring hard enough at the screen. Jack watched both of them and understood that truth arriving late was still heavy when it came through the door.

After the television went dark, Mary opened the ledger to the old pages from 1969. Funeral. Sirens. First board. First nail. Then she turned to a clean line and wrote what the storm had returned.

She did not try to make it pretty. Water tried to take the field, she wrote. It gave back a gun instead.

Outside, Cedarbrook was a mess of mud and torn grass and washed-out chalk. But the posts along the creek still stood where they had stood before the rain decided to remember.

Chapter Fourteen — February 1978: The Blizzard

©

(February 1978 · Saugus, Massachusetts)

WBZ 1030, 6:02 A. m.:

"Two, maybe three feet before this is over..."

The announcer's voice crackled around the edges, but the words were clear. "We're talking about a storm with a long memory, folks. If you can stay put, stay put. Check on neighbors. We'll keep you company."

Mary had the radio wedged between the coffee pot and the ledger. Outside the kitchen window, snow already blurred the world into three shades of white. The bare maple in the front yard dragged its branches, scraping at the sky.

She drew a quick list on the pad beside the ledger:

Fosters—older. Shallow driveway. Mrs. Romano—heart. Stairs.

Parker—says he doesn't need it, gets one anyway.

George set his mug down with a soft clink.

"I should be at the plant," he said.

"Pipes will freeze. They'll need hands."

"Hands can't do anything from a ditch on 1A,"

Mary answered.

"Doctor said your lungs don't need a blizzard on top of everything else."

"I'm fine," he said, then coughed hard enough to argue with himself. Jack sat at the table, lacing his boots.

"I'll go look before it gets bad," he said.

"Field, creek, neighbors.

You can see the storm from the porch now. It's already here."

Mary studied him a moment—the boy she still saw layered under the broad-shouldered young man in front of her. He was nearly as tall as George now, arms roped from work instead of just growth spurts.

"Check your own feet first," she said.

"You step into a drift past your waist, you turn around. The field will still be there tomorrow. People might not."

She flipped to a fresh page in the ledger and wrote, quick and neat: Entry #78—When the world disappears, start with the square of porch you can clear.

By mid-morning, the storm had swallowed the neighborhood. Snow didn't fall straight down; it came in sideways sheets, driven by a wind that sounded like it had bones to grind. The sky was the same color as the ground. The horizon disappeared. The maple in the yard bent toward the marsh, branches loaded and creaking.

Mary nudged the radio volume up.

"Visibility near zero on Route 1," the announcer said later that morning. "Police urge drivers to abandon cars if they're stuck and seek shelter.

Again, if you can stay home, stay home. Check on your elderly neighbors. This one's for the record books."

The house felt smaller with every update. Usual sounds, the fridge hum, the ticking clock—seemed louder, like the walls were listening.

In the front hall, Jack layered a second pair of socks and tugged a hat down over his ears.

"I'll test it," he said.

"Just the porch."

Mary opened the door. The storm pushed back, cold and white and heavy. Snow had drifted up over the first step. Jack shoved his boot into it and felt it swallow his leg up to the knee.

"That's as far as you go alone," George said.

By afternoon, Saugus had turned into a maze of trenches.

Neighbors formed shoveling brigades, carving narrow canyons from doorways to the main paths. Teenagers did the heaviest lifting, cutting tunnels between houses and clearing ledges off older folks' steps.

"Start at the Fosters',"

Mary told Jack, pressing a thermos into his hands. "They've got half the town's coffee trapped in there."

"Romano's next,"

George added.

"Can't have this place snowed in without sauce."

At the Romano house, the front door opened onto a solid wall of snow. It took four kids and forty minutes to dig a passage deep enough for Mrs. Romano to squeeze through.

She emerged with a scarf around her hair and steam fogging her glasses, thrusting a pot toward them.

"Take this," she said.

"Give everyone a ladle and tell them there's more on the stove."

"What is it?" one boy asked.

"Does it matter?" she said.

"It's hot. It's food. Move." At Mrs.

Foster's, the back way was the only way.

Jack and two others dug down and around until they found the cellar bulkhead. Kay met them in a cloud of coffee steam.

"You kids are out of your minds," she said.

"Get inside before you freeze your faces off."

"We've got more to dig,"

Jack said.

She shoved a box of day-olds into his arms.

"Then take these," she said.

"Free. And if anyone argues, tell them the blizzard put everything on sale."

They laughed and trudged back into the trench.

As they worked, Cedarbrook lay somewhere under the drifted white— fence, backstop, and infield all swallowed by the storm's equalizer. The line between field and marsh disappeared under a single smooth blanket.

But the kids knew where it was.

After they cleared the most important paths—from the oldest neighbors' doors to the main route, they turned their shovels toward the field.

"Why?" one asked.

"Nobody's playing anything today."

Jack jabbed his shovel into the snow where the third-base line would be.

"Because when this melts, we're going to need a place to stand," he said.

"And because if the fence could hold the flood, the least we can do is make sure it can breathe in this."

They dug a narrow corridor along the inside of the fence, carving out a shallow trench where water could run when the thaw came. It was the mirror image of what they'd done during the flood, different season, same instinct.

At one point, Jack looked up, panting, and realized he could only see the tops of the posts.

"Looks like it's drowning," Kevin said beside him. "Looks like it's still here,"

Jack answered.

By the time the worst passed, the blizzard had a name and a slot in every newscast.

Anchors talked about records falling and cars abandoned, about neighbors pulling each other out—shovels, snowblowers, even one guy with a rope tied to his living room couch. One segment showed a grainy shot of Cedarbrook: kids with shovels, a line of posts half-buried but bright against the snowbank.

"Here in Saugus," the reporter said, "families at the Cedarbrook neighborhood field spent the day digging paths not just for themselves but for each other.

They've been fighting to keep this field untouched by development for years. Today, it helped keep the town moving."

The phrase the station liked to use—Spirit of New England—floated out again, but it landed differently this time. It didn't sound like a slogan. It sounded earned.

In the Davis living room, everyone watched the clip in wavering blue light.

"That our fence?"

George asked. "That's our fence,"

Jack said.

Mary didn't answer. Her hand went to the ledger.

Entry #70—Storm Test #2: Snow buried the field, but the kids dug each other out.

The fence didn't move. Neither did they.

Beneath it, smaller:

Entry #71—WBZ called it the 'Spirit of New England.' For once, the words fit.

She closed the book.

Outside, the storm finally began to ease. Wind lost its bite. Snow settled into something you could live with instead of something that wanted you gone.

The trenches the kids had dug looked like small, determined rivers cut into the white. When spring came, the water would know where to go.

Later, when the last of the drifts shrank back from the rails, Jack and Mary stood together at the back window.

The fence ran in a dark, uneven line through the lingering snow, a scar, a signature, a sentence that refused to be buried.

"Think it's straight enough?" Jack asked.

Mary watched the way the rails rose and dipped where the storm had leaned hardest.

"After a week like this?" she said.

"Straight enough to hold."

Somewhere beyond the plowed piles, beyond the stalled cars and frozen neon of Route 1, the ocean breathed in and out, indifferent.

The fence didn't know that. It only knew where it stood.

(Late February 1978 · Cedarbrook Field)

The snow had stopped falling, but it had not stopped deciding where it wanted to live. It drifted against the fence in high white shoulders. George shoveled in silence, each scrape of metal on packed snow a kind of prayer. Jack worked beside him, younger muscles burning with the need to prove they could do what older men did.

Mary stood near the backstop with a thermos and her hands tucked into her coat sleeves, watching the way George's breath came a little shorter than it used to.

"Take a break," she called.

George did not answer. He shoved again.

Then the shovel stopped. Not because the snow was stubborn.

Because George's body was.

He straightened slowly, one hand braced on the handle, the other pressing into his chest as if he could hold something in place by force.

Jack froze. "George?"

George tried to wave it off. His mouth opened and no sound came out. The world narrowed—snow, fence, the dark line of trees, Mary's face suddenly pale.

Mary crossed the field fast, boots slipping. She caught George's elbow. His skin through the coat felt cold in a way that was not February.

"Do not," he said, and it was the most frightened word she had ever heard him say. "Do not make a scene."

"This is not a scene,"

Mary said.

"This is your heart."

George swallowed. His pride fought his fear. "If I go," he whispered, "they will say the field is unsafe. They will say I am not fit. They will say -"

"Let them say whatever they want,"

Mary said, tightening her grip. "You do not get to die to make them comfortable."

Jack stood a step away, helpless with love and terror, watching them argue with his father's body.

Mary turned her face toward the road. "Go get the car," she told Jack. "Now."

Jack ran, snow spraying behind him.

George met Mary's eyes and gave the smallest nod. It was not surrender. It was trust.

"I am sorry,"

George breathed, as if apologizing for being human. "Do not be sorry,"

Mary whispered.

"Be here."

Chapter Fifteen — The Closed-Door Vote

©

(Late Winter 1978 · Saugus Town Hall)

THE MEETING EVERYONE TALKED about wasn't the first meeting. It was just the first one the town admitted to.

Three nights before the vote, Mary found herself outside the municipal building with the ledger tucked under her coat and a cold that had nothing to do with weather tightening her ribs.

The hallways smelled like floor wax and old paper. A man in a janitor's uniform nodded at her without interest—people rarely looked twice at a woman carrying a book. They assumed it was harmless.

From behind a closed door, voices rose and fell. Not shouting—worse. Calm. The kind of calm that meant decisions had already been made and now they were simply being justified.

Mary paused. She heard Hartwell's name once, then Parker Greene's, then the phrase "liability exposure" spoken with the certainty of natural law.

She pressed her ear closer to the door. One of the voices belonged to Councilman Forni. She knew his tone from the diner, from Little League fundraisers, from the way he'd once told George, "Good fence. Keeps the kids honest."

"We can't keep kicking the can," Forni said now. "The refinery brings jobs. Real ones. And if we don't take it, someone else will."

"Someone else already is," another man replied.

"Providence's numbers assume access. They assume the creek frontage. They assume we can clear the recreational designation."

A third voice—lower, careful. "And if we can't?"

"Then we make it about safety," Forni said.

"You want to beat a mother? You don't argue money. You argue risk."

Mary felt her stomach drop. Safety. The word that could muzzle any room.

"There's a kid injury file," the careful voice continued.

"Minor stuff. Broken wrist. Cut lip. But we can frame it."

Mary pictured Jack's scraped knees, the kind he'd come home with grinning, proud from the small wars of childhood. She pictured those scabs turned into exhibits.

A chair scraped. Paper rustled. Then Forni again, quieter. "Look, I'm not proud of it. But the town needs to move forward. We can't be held hostage by nostalgia."

Nostalgia. Mary almost laughed. She thought of George's hands, of Michael's letters, of Fred's fence posts driven into frozen ground. If that was nostalgia, then nostalgia was a kind of labor.

She stepped back before anger made her careless. The hallway light buzzed. Her breath sounded loud.

Across the corridor, a door opened. Parker Greene came out, alone, fixing his tie like it was a wound. He froze when he saw her.

"Mary," he said.

She didn't pretend she was lost.

Pretending was for people who wanted to be forgiven. "They're going to make it about safety," she said.

Parker's eyes flicked to the closed door. He didn't deny it. That was the worst part.

"They're scared," he said.

"And Hartwell knows how to use it."

"So do you,"

Mary replied.

Parker flinched, but he didn't fight her. "You want to win?" he asked.

"Then don't let them turn your field into a hazard report."

Mary tightened her grip on the ledger. "How?"

Parker exhaled. "Get ahead of it. Bring witnesses. Bring the kids. Bring the parents. And—"

He hesitated. "There's a paper. A signature."

Mary's heart kicked. "Whose?"

Parker looked past her, down the hall. "Somebody who thinks they're saving you," he said.

"Somebody you trust."

Mary felt the hallway tilt.

Trust was the only currency Hartwell couldn't print—so, of course, he was trying to counterfeit it.

"Tomorrow,"

Parker added.

"They're going to lock in their story before the town hears yours."

Mary nodded once. The calm settled over her—not peaceful, not resigned. The calm of a woman who understood that a fight was a schedule, not a moment.

She turned to go, then stopped. "Parker," she said.

"Yeah?"

"When you say 'the town,' "

Mary told him, "try to remember it has faces."

Parker's mouth tightened. "I know," he said. But his eyes didn't look convinced.

Outside, the air cut clean across her cheeks. George waited by the car, hands on the steering wheel as if he could keep the night from sliding away.

Mary got in and didn't speak for a full minute. George didn't press. That was one of the ways he loved her—by making room for what she couldn't say yet.

When she finally turned to him, she reached across the seat and rested her hand on his. His fingers curled around hers like a decision.

"They're going to come for us with safety," she whispered. George nodded once. "Then we go in with truth," he said.

George lifted her hand and pressed his lips to her knuckles—quick, almost shy. Mary almost laughed.

"We hold the line," George said.

"We hold each other," Mary corrected.

And for the first time in days, George smiled like he believed they might.

Chapter Sixteen — The Town Meeting

©

(Late 1978 · Saugus, Massachusetts)

WBZ WAS ALREADY ON the story before they left the house.

The radio talked about Article 17 like it was a zoning question. Mary knew better. It was a naming question. The town would decide whether Cedarbrook was memory, nuisance, or room to breathe.

Jack wore a dress shirt that made him feel borrowed from somebody older. George lost a fight with his tie. Mary packed the ledger, the petitions, and the pages she had marked with tabs until the book looked less like a diary than a case file.

"You sure you want me there?" Jack asked.

"They're not voting on my childhood,"

Mary said.

"Or your father's. They're voting on yours. So yes."

Town Hall filled early. Folding chairs scraped. Radiators hissed. People shuffled bright maps that made the marsh look clean enough to sell.

Hartwell sat in the second row with his papers stacked precisely, as if order itself were proof of virtue.

When the moderator called his name, he rose in the smooth, public way of a man used to being mistaken for reasonable.

He spoke about modernization, fiscal responsibility, broadening the tax base, jobs. Always jobs. He talked about roads and public safety and reduced Cedarbrook to a colored block on a map so small it could be covered by a thumb.

"We respect the town's history," he said at the close. "We are simply asking you to help it move forward."

The applause he got was polite and thin. Parker stood without notes.

"I'm not against jobs," he said.

"I'm against pretending we don't know what this piece of ground is."

He pointed not at the map, but toward the back of the room, toward the neighborhood beyond it. "That field has already paid taxes the town never counted. It has paid in grief carried there, boys raised there, and trouble absorbed there instead of on a road."

The room loosened around the edges. People laughed once when he said Parcel E like it was a bad joke and then stopped laughing when he said, "Some lines you do not move. You build around them."

A teacher spoke after him. Then a man from the hardware store. Then two parents Mary knew only by first names and the way their children ran.

When the moderator found her, Mary stood with the ledger already open.

"I keep records," she said.

"Some of you know that."

She lifted the book just high enough for people to see what it was. "I have written down what this field has cost this town—meetings, fines, warnings, repairs, threats dressed up as policy. I have also written down what it has given us."

Now she looked directly at Hartwell.

"It gave us a place to grieve after the Red Coach killings when every radio in town sounded like bad news. It gave our kids a place to go where the lesson wasn't buy something, break something, or get out of the way. When the flood came, it gave back a gun and with it a truth this town had been carrying around in its chest for nearly a decade."

Nobody moved.

"You call this progress because the paper is clean,"

Mary said.

"I'm asking you to look at what has already held here without a brochure. Tonight you get to decide whether this town still recognizes one of its own lines when it sees it."

The applause after that came rougher and louder, the kind that sounded less like approval than relief.

Debate continued because rooms like that always insisted on procedure after truth had already done its work. Amendments were offered. Questions were raised. The moderator bought everybody a few more minutes of pretending the result was still unwritten.

When he finally called the vote, the room went tight. Hands rose for rezoning. Then more hands rose against it.

Jack snapped his pencil before the moderator finished counting. "Article 17 fails," the clerk announced.

For one beat the room did not trust itself to believe it. Then the noise came—cheers, claps, a few relieved shouts. Hartwell gathered his papers the way men gather things when they have lost in public and want it to look temporary.

Later, when the house went quiet, Mary stood at the back window with the ledger open on the table behind her. Outside, the fence looked exactly as it had that morning.

She wrote the result in a steady hand and allowed herself six private words in the margin: Ground beat map. Tonight, that was enough.

Chapter Seventeen — The First Summer Without

©

Flags

(Summer 1979 · The Creek Field · Saugus, Massachusetts) Survey paint faded first.

The red lines Hartwell's men had sprayed along the marsh went chalkpink, then ghosted out under rain and sun. The little plastic flags that once snapped in the wind lost their color, leaned. And finally broke at the soil line. Kids hooked the loose ones with their toes and sent them skidding down the hill like bright, useless minnows.

No trucks came. No surveyors. No suits.

By June, the only lines that mattered again were the ones the kids drew with their cleats.

Morning games started early that first summer. Jack woke to the sound of aluminum ping and wooden crack, the thud of a ball into somebody's overworked glove, laughing arguments about whether a shot to the right-field corner was fair or foul. From the kitchen window, Mary could see clusters of kids in mismatched uniforms spreading across the outfield like bright coins tossed onto green felt. The fence had gone back to being background—a silver-brown spine holding the hill. Boards still bore hammer scars and pencil marks from the winter work. But the yellow NO TRESPASSING signs Hartwell had tried to hang never went up. The only sign on the backstop now was the one the town had agreed on in a packed room with bad coffee and folded chairs:

CEDARBROOK FIELD

Parker said it every time he came by with a rake over his shoulder. "Look at that," he'd murmur. "Field again. Not a target."

He'd take a slow lap, running his hand along the outfield boards.

George didn't walk as quickly as he used to, but he made his rounds. He'd stand by the gate, watching a game play out, seeing every bad hop the way a carpenter sees a nail he never quite trusted. When Jack wandered over between innings, George would nod once, small and satisfied, like a man checking a line with his eye and finding it true.

"Flags are gone,"

Jack said once, shading his eyes toward the marsh. "They weren't the line,"

George answered.

"This is."

He tapped the nearest post with his knuckles, lightly, almost tenderly.

Dedication Day

The plaque went into the ground on a warm Sunday two weeks after the town meeting.

They called it Dedication Day, because "We Didn't Let Them Take It" wouldn't fit on the flyer.

Cars lined both sides of Chestnut Street. People who hadn't been to a game in years came and stood along the hill in church clothes and work boots, sunglasses and ball caps, arms folded or hands shoved deep into pockets. Some came out of guilt, some out of pride, most because they'd told themselves I ought to be there and finally listened.

Father Duffy wore his collar and his old Red Sox cap, the one he insisted wasn't technically part of his vestments but had "seen enough last-inning prayers to qualify." He stood by the third-base line with a small book in one hand and the other resting on the new stone marker waiting to be unveiled.

Mary had argued for the wording and won most of it:

CEDARBROOK FIELD

In memory of those we lost and those who refused to look away. Saugus, Massachusetts

No names, but everyone saw faces when they read it—Forni, Belmonte, the men who never came home from Da Nang, the families who'd had to drive past the Red Coach Grill parking lot and pretend they didn't see the dark shape in memory.

The town manager said a few words about "community" and "democracy in action." A councilor who had changed his vote at the last minute spoke about "listening to the people." His voice wobbled when he got to that part; Mary watched him and wondered if he'd ever understand exactly what it had almost cost.

Parker's remarks were shorter.

He stepped up, cleared his throat once, and nodded toward the hill.

"Lot of folks in this town know how to tear things down," he said.

"Fewer know how to build something and stand in front of it when trouble comes. You all chose the second thing. That's what this is."

He pointed his chin toward the kids sprawled along the baselines. "And they're the reason."

He stepped back before anyone could clap too much for him, letting the sound drift downhill toward George.

When it was Father Duffy's turn, he lifted his cap, bowed his head for a moment, then looked out over the field.

"Bless this ground, Lord," he said.

"Bless the boards that keep the worst of the world out and the chalk that tells these kids where to run. Bless the hands that swing the hammers, the backs that rake the infield, and the people who show up long after their own kids are grown. May this place remember who we are when we forget. Amen."

"Amen," the hill answered, a little louder than he'd expected.

After the cloth came off the plaque, Mary circulated with a coffee urn and a tray of paper cups. She moved through the clusters the way she had during petition days, except now people stepped toward her instead of away.

"You did it, Mary," one woman said.

"We just signed."

"You signing was the doing,"

Mary replied, and left it there. Parker leaned over as she passed him near the third-base line.

"Thought you didn't like being the center of attention," he said.

"I don't," she said, adjusting the tray. "That's why I keep putting a fence between me and it."

He barked out a laugh. Father Duffy, standing nearby, shook his head.

"You're going to guilt-trip people into heaven," he told her. "Just doing my part, Father," she said.

"Same as you."

The Space Trouble Left

By July, the field had settled into a new normal. The survey flags were gone. The refinery men stayed on the far side of Route 1, their project tied up in courtrooms and ledgers instead of mud and marsh. Winter Hill had found other corners to darken.

The absence of danger left a kind of hollow in the air at Cedarbrook— a space where fear had stood for months. The town did what towns do when a space like that opens up.

It filled it with kids.

Little brothers got dragged into games they weren't ready for yet, tripping over their feet in right field, proud just to be out there. Older girls took over the hill above first base, timing their conversations to the crack of the bat. Fathers who had sworn they were done with youth sports found themselves drawn to the backstop after dinner, fingers curling through the chain link as if it were rosary.

Sometimes, in the shade along the third-base side, you could still hear Article 17 muttered like a bad memory.

"Imagine if they'd paved it," someone would say.

"Don't," another would answer. "We didn't, and that's the point."

George tried not to count how many boards he'd replaced or how many nails he'd driven. His body was doing that for him—lungs catching sooner on the hill, hands stiffening after long days. He kept the worry mostly to himself.

"You all right?"

Jack asked once as they walked home, gloves hooked over their shoulders. "Fence is straight,"

George answered.

"Everything else we'll see about."

It wasn't the answer to the question Jack had asked, but it was the one George had to give.

Michael Comes Home

Michael came home for good that summer, thinner than he'd gone and older around the eyes.

The notice from the Army had arrived two weeks before: rotation finished, paperwork cleared. The day he stepped off the bus on Western Avenue, there were no bands, no speeches. Just Mary, George. And Jack waiting by the curb, all three trying not to stare at the duffel that looked too light.

Mary reached for him first. He hugged her with one arm, the other hanging at his side as if it hadn't quite remembered what to do yet. George waited until Mary let go, then stepped in and held his son for a long, wordless count of ten.

Jack's hug came last, awkward and fierce, the way only a kid's can be when he's waited years for that hug.

"You're taller,"

Michael said.

"You're skinnier,"

Jack answered.

They both pretended that was all that had changed.

That night, after the first round of home-cooked food and the fifth time someone almost said Red Coach and didn't, Michael went outside "for some air." Mary let him go. She watched from the kitchen window as he walked up the hill alone, hands shoved in his jacket pockets despite the warm weather.

He stopped at the top of Cedarbrook, just behind the backstop, and stood there for a long time.

The field below was half-lit by streetlamps and porch light. A few kids were still out, lingering over one last inning in the dim, their voices low and tired. The fence traced a dark line around them, steady as a heartbeat.

Michael rested his palm against one of the posts. He didn't lean on it; he just touched the wood as if taking a pulse.

He could see, in flashes, a different field half a world away—no boards, no chalk, just red dust and noise and the ache of waiting for something you couldn't see coming. The contrast made his throat tighten. "How's it look?" Jack's voice came from halfway down the hill.

Michael didn't turn right away.

"Straight," he said finally. "Better than I deserve."

Jack came to stand beside him. They stayed that way for a minute—two silhouettes at the top of the hill, watching younger kids play the same games they'd played, on ground that had almost been turned into something else entirely.

"George is gonna try to keep up with it,"

Jack said.

"Parker too."

Michael nodded.

"Won't all be on them," he said.

"Not anymore."

Mary watched them from the window and saw it clearly: Michael and Jack framed by the boards Fred had started, George had carried. And Parker had held in place when it mattered. The line looked solid, but she could feel the weight of it leaning against her own spine.

Later, after the lights were out and the radios had gone quiet up and down the street, she sat at the table with the ledger open in front of her. The kitchen smelled like dish soap and oregano, like a Sunday that had gone too late and turned into Monday.

She turned back through the ledger—petitions, Article 17, the busing year, the flood, the blizzard. Each entry felt like another hand braced against the same post.

At a clean page near the back, she uncapped her pen and wrote:

Entry #80—First Summer Without Flags, 1979.

Too much weight on one post.

Hand it down before it breaks.

She let the ink dry and closed the ledger.

Outside, the creek moved in the dark and the fence held. Trouble was still there; it had merely given the children a season's head start.

Chapter Eighteen — The Hand-Off

©

(Spring 1981 · Chestnut Street / The Creek Field)

BY THE SPRING OF 1981, Jack could throw harder than most of the men who'd taught him.

He was nineteen now. His shoulders had gone broad from shovels, hammers, and long toss. His forearms carried the ropey look of someone who'd spent more time with tools and baseballs than notebooks. College coaches had started appearing along the baselines, hats low, clipboards propped against their chests. A scout or two from further away had leaned on the fence on Saturdays, sunglasses on even when the sky was overcast.

Scholarships were whispered about. So were places far from Route 1.

The fence didn't care about any of that. It still needed boards replaced.

New Boards

"Hold it steady," Parker said.

Jack pressed the fresh two-by-six against the post, shoulder firm to the grain. The cut wood smell rose in his nose—sharp, clean, nothing like the musty boards they'd pulled off and stacked to the side.

The old plank lay in the grass, split where years of kids had sat between innings, where winter had forced water into every hairline crack and pried it open.

Parker set the first nail, gave it two quick taps to bite, then handed Jack the hammer.

"Your turn," he said.

"Man of the hour."

Jack smirked.

"I thought you said this field doesn't need heroes," he answered.

"Doesn't,"

Parker said.

"Needs stewards."

Jack drove the nail in, the head sinking flush with the wood in five solid strokes. The sound rang up into his arm—an echo he'd known since he was small enough to watch Fred swing from the safety of the porch.

They worked their way down the row like that: Parker setting, Jack driving.

The rhythm settled into something comfortable—hammer, breath, small adjustment, hammer again.

"So,"

Parker said after a while, not looking up from the nail he was placing. "All these fellas with clipboards. They see a kid or a fence?"

"Both,"

Jack said.

"I think."

"Funny thing about fences,"

Parker went on. "Nobody notices 'em when they're where they belong. Only time folks stare is when one's missing or crooked."

He straightened, stretching his back until it popped.

"This whole town's been staring at this line for ten years," he said.

"Not because it's pretty. Because it stayed."

Jack set his foot on the bottom rail, testing the new plank with a small push. "What happens when I'm not here?" he asked before he could talk himself out of it. "If I go. College. Whatever."

Parker squinted down the length of the boards, eyeing the way they met at the next post.

"Same thing that happened when Fred wasn't here anymore," he said.

"Somebody else picks up the hammer. Question ain't whether you stay. It's what you leave straight enough for the next set of hands."

He turned, studied Jack for a second.

"You're not the fence,"

Parker said.

"You're just the next man making sure it doesn't sag."

Jack looked out at the field.

Kids were running a scrimmage—too many in the outfield, not enough behind the plate, a mess of arms and legs and yells that would have driven a perfectionist crazy. It made his chest ache with a kind of rough affection.

"George gonna be all right?" he asked quietly. Parker wiped sawdust on his pants.

"Man's carried more than most," he said.

"Body's gonna have its say whether he wants it to or not."

He nodded toward the house on Chestnut Street.

"Doesn't all have to ride him anymore, though. Or Mary."

Jack hit the last nail a little harder than he meant to. The board settled firm against the post. Parker stepped back, checked the line one more time, and grunted approval.

"Good," he said.

"You'll do." Entry #100

That night the ledger lay open under the reading lamp, its spine tired but unwilling to quit.

Mary turned through the pages not to revisit them, but to feel their weight in order: Hartwell's first visit. Article 17 underlined twice. The flood. The gun. The blizzard. Names of boys who had grown into shoulders and then into men. George's cough, written small on days she did not want the page to make it real.

The book was nearly out of room. She had known for weeks that the next line needed to be hers and the one after that needed not to be.

She uncapped the pen and wrote carefully:

Entry #100—Ten years since the Red Coach Grill. Fear loud. Faith tested. Flood, blizzard, votes, and whispered threats. The fence still stands. Kids still play.

That was enough. Anything prettier would have been vanity.

She closed the ledger, rested her hand on it a moment, and then took a plain brown notebook from the sideboard drawer.

Jack was still awake when she knocked on his door. "Can't sleep?" she asked.

He gave the kind of shrug boys use when their thoughts have gotten too big for the room. "Games. Schools. Futures."

Mary set the new notebook on his desk and laid the old ledger on top of it.

"You retiring?" he asked, trying for a joke and not quite landing it. "From writing things down? No," she said.

"From writing this part down? Yes."

She slid the ledger toward him.

"This is the story of the fence," she said.

"Fred's, George's, mine.

The part where the town kept trying to forget what it already knew."

His fingertips touched the worn cover. It looked like a book. It felt like a tool.

"Read it,"

Mary said.

"Not all tonight. Enough to know where the line came from."

He nodded toward the blank notebook beneath it. "And that one?" Mary pushed the new notebook forward.

"That one's yours." He waited.

"Your mess," she said.

"And your record."

A breath escaped him that was almost a laugh. "What if I don't know what to write first?"

Mary put the pen beside the notebook. "Start with whatever made you stay."

She stood, smoothing her apron. At the doorway she paused just long enough to make sure he had really put his hand on the cover.

When she left, Jack opened the blank book and sat with the page a while before the first sentence came.

"Jack," she said.

He looked up.

"You're not being handed a burden," she said.

"You're being handed a chance not to let what other people built go crooked. There's a difference."

He nodded. She left the door open a crack.

Jack sat for a long moment, listening to the house settle again.

Then he picked up the pen.

His handwriting had grown more confident over the years but still carried a hint of the twelve-year-old who'd first traced his name in the dirt behind home plate. He wrote slowly, the way he did when he wanted his catcher to see the sign and not miss it.

Entry #101—This field was not a gift. It was something people paid for with sleep, blood, and a lot of nails. My job isn't to own it.

My job is to keep the line straight and leave room for the next kids to run.

He stared at the words. They weren't perfect. They were his.

Jack closed the notebook and set it on top of the old ledger. The two together looked less like a weight now and more like a bridge.

The Line Outside

Later, in the dark, he lay in bed and listened to the familiar sounds.

A car turning the corner at the bottom of the hill. A dog barking twice, then thinking better of it. Somewhere, a radio fading out a latenight game, the announcer's voice blurring into static and then gone.

Behind all of it, under it, was the constant whisper of the creek. It had carried glass and a gun and any number of secrets over the years. Now it carried spring runoff and the faint echoes of kids' shouts from the afternoon.

He turned toward the window.

Through the thin curtain he could see the suggestion of the fence—dark uprights against a slightly lighter sky, boards running in a line his grandfather had started and strangers had tried to bend. For the first time, he didn't feel like the kid standing on the wrong side of it, waiting to be let in. He felt like someone standing beside it, one hand on the wood, watching which way the world tried to push.

He exhaled, long and slow.

The world beyond Route 1 might want him. Scouts might have plans. Coaches might have opinions about his arm, his future, his worth.

The fence outside didn't have an opinion. It just needed tending.

Knowing where his line was, Jack closed his eyes and finally slept.

Epilogue — The Fence in Spring

©

WBZ 1030 SIGNED OFF the old-fashioned way that night.

"It's eleven fifty-eight on the North Shore," the voice said, mellow and familiar. "This is WBZ Boston, your Spirit of New England. Good night."

The last chord of some soft rock ballad drifted under the words and faded. Mary reached over and turned the radio down to a murmur, then off. The sudden quiet in the kitchen felt both strange and earned.

The ledger sat open in front of her, its spine protesting after so many years of being bent flat. Beside it lay Jack's new notebook, closed, a pen resting on top. She had resisted the urge to peek.

Instead, she let her fingers travel over her own pages one last time.

Here was the entry where Fred's blood and her prayers had first met on paper. Here, the early guesses at Hartwell's intentions—too generous, she saw now. Here, the first whispered mention of Winter Hill and the phone numbers Parker had slid across her table with hands that wouldn't quite stop shaking.

Flood water had blurred these lines; blizzard cold had made these letters jagged. Some pages were almost beautiful in their neatness, written on rare quiet days when grief and fear had given her a moment's distance.

She flipped past the trooper names, the council votes, the busing hearings where Boston burned on TV while the boys from the block did their homework. Past the flood and the gun. Past the February when the town dug itself out shoulder to shoulder. Past the town meeting where Article 17 finally broke under the weight of its own lies. Past the day the plaque went into the ground and trouble had to move down the road to find a foothold.

Past the entry she'd written tonight—Entry #100–still drying near the back.

Her hand rested in the narrow space beneath it, the last empty lines she'd decided to leave alone.

For a long time she sat there, listening to the house breathe.

George wheezed once in his sleep down the hall and settled. Jack turned over in his room, the bedsprings giving a soft complaint. Somewhere outside, a car door shut, a porch light clicked off, the neighborhood closing itself up for the night.

Mary uncapped her pen one more time.

She didn't move to the center of the page. Instead, she bent close and wrote in the bottom margin, in letters small and sure:

Still here. So are we. She set the pen down.

The words weren't a prayer, exactly. They weren't a boast either. They were a simple, stubborn report from the front line she'd helped draw.

Mary closed the ledger gently, then slid it beneath Jack's notebook so the newer, lighter thing sat on top.

Wood and water and ink, past and future, all in one small stack on a scarred kitchen table. She turned off the lamp and stepped out onto the back stoop.

The air had that early-spring bite—sharp enough to remind you winter wasn't finished, soft enough to hint it soon would be. Down the hill, the creek whispered over stones, swollen but contained. The fence stood between the water and the houses, boards dark and solid in the moonlight.

She could trace, in her mind, every hand that had lifted those boards. Fred's. George's. Parker's. Jack's. The boys who'd leaned there to watch older kids play, the mothers who'd rested a hand there when they laughed or cried on long afternoons.

Mary folded her arms against the chill and took it in—not as a monument, but as a job still in progress.

"Still here," she said softly into the dark.

The fence didn't answer. It just held its line—exactly what she'd always asked of it.

She stayed a moment longer, listening to the creek and the quiet houses and the faint, imagined echo of a ball hitting leather somewhere in the near future.

Then she went inside and closed the door.

A Note on the Series

The Sandlot Promise is Book One of The Sandlot Series.

The Sandlot Series can be read in publication order, beginning here, or in story chronology, beginning with Beneath the Home Run Sky, the prequel that tells the earlier story of Fred Davis, George Davis, Mary Davis, Cedarbrook Field, and the first lines pulled across the dirt.

The Sandlot Promise begins in the winter of 1969-70, after the night of December 27, 1969, when the lives of two Saugus families changed in a parking lot off Route 1. Officer Arthur Belmonte was killed in the line of duty that night. Officer Frederick Forni was wounded and survived. Their families have given me their permission to refer to them by name. The book is dedicated to them.

The Sandlot Legacy is Book Two. It follows George Davis, Cedarbrook Field, and Jack Thompson through the years when the field's future is challenged and its meaning is tested.

The Sandlot Spirit is Book Three. It picks up the same field a generation later, as the Ruggiero family navigates what youth baseball has become.

Together, the books follow one promise across generations: a field, a fence, and the people who keep showing up when the game needs adults worthy of it.

— W. A. B.

Continue the Series

Return to the origin in Beneath the Home Run Sky, a Sandlot Series Prequel, where Fred Davis, George Davis, Mary Davis, and Cedarbrook Field first begin to take shape.

Then continue forward in The Sandlot Legacy, Book Two of The Sandlot Series—set a decade later, when the field's future hangs in the balance and Mary's ledger becomes the record of what a town will and won't let go of.

www.ingramcontent.com/pod-product-compliance
Lightning Source LLC
LaVergne TN
LVHW040221110826
845146LV00005B/1364

* 9 7 9 8 9 8 8 8 4 4 8 5 3 *